D0446323

THE SPY IN A BOX

RALPH DENNIS

BRASH
BOOKS

Copyright © 2020 Adventures in Television, Inc.
All rights reserved.

The characters and events portrayed in this book are fictitious. Any similarity to real persons, living or dead, is coincidental and not intended by the author.

No part of this book may be reproduced, or stored in a retrieval system, or transmitted in any form or by any means, electronic, mechanical, photocopying, recording, or otherwise, without express written permission of the publisher.

ISBN: 1941298893
ISBN-13: 978-1-941298-89-3

Published by
Brash Books, LLC
12120 State Line #253
Leawood, Kansas 66209
www.brash-books.com

RECEIVED

DEC 2 1 2019

NO LONGER PROPERTY OF
SOUTHWEST BRANCH
SEATTLE PUBLIC LIBRARY

THE SPY IN A BOX

NO LONGER PROPERTY OF
SEATTLE PUBLIC LIBRARY

Also by Ralph Dennis
The War Heist
A Talent for Killing
The Broken Fixer
Dust in the Heart

The Hardman Series
Atlanta Deathwatch
The Charleston Knife is Back in Town
Golden Girl And All
Pimp For The Dead
Down Among The Jocks
Murder Is Not An Odd Job
Working For The Man
Deadly Cotton Heart
The One Dollar Rip-Off
Hump's First Case
The Last Of The Armageddon Wars
The Buy Back Blues

PUBLISHER'S NOTE

Author Ralph Dennis is best known for his ground-breaking *Hardman* series, twelve crime novels set in Atlanta in the 1970s. He died in 1988, leaving behind several unpublished manuscripts. *The Spy in a Box* is one of those manuscripts.

CHAPTER ONE

December, 1980

It was not as easy as it had once been, setting up the meeting with Paul Marcos. San Nicolas, the capitol city of Costa Verde, was bubbling, near the boiling point and the top of the pot was about to blow away. The city was full of watchers, the "eyes" of a dozen organizations that wanted control of Costa Verde when the promised free elections were held in January, hardly a month away. A man in Will Hall's position, the Company Man in shallow cover as a cultural attaché, had to prejudge every move he made. He knew that each faction in Costa Verde would understand or misunderstand that move in terms of their own goals.

For the past month, Will Hall had used the coded wires and the diplomatic pouches to argue that the U.S. should support the moderate wing. Otherwise, he said, wins by either of the extremes, the rebels backed by Cuba or the right wing supported by the old landowners and the mining interests, would lead to a bloodbath and terrible repression.

The moderate faction, headed by Paul Marcos, had assured him that his party would accomodate elements from both extremes in his government. Terror and repression would be avoided, Marcos promised Hall.

It was the only solution, Hall believed. For a time, he even thought he might have influenced the Company. But this morning, while Hall ate a late breakfast, the message was received from Washington. It was delivered to Hall by a Marine guard while he sat over a third cup of coffee and a cigarette.

Enough about Paul M.

Reports noted and studied. Contact Valdez.

Shiner

It was difficult, on short notice, to set up a secret meeting with Marcos. Now it was necessary. The order that he contact Valdez, second in command of the right-wing element, placed Hall in a bad position. He owed Marcos an explanation. Otherwise the meeting with Valdez might be misunderstood. Even the moderate wing had their "eyes" about the city.

In another time, or another city, he might have used the phone. In Costa Verde, the state controlled the phone system. The Embassy phones were definitely not secure. And it was a thousand to one bet that Paul's home phone and the one at the moderate party offices were bugged as well.

It would have to be an unscheduled meeting with Marcos. That was the only way. Once that was decided, Will Hall shuffled papers in his office on the third floor of the Embassy until 11:30 and then he rode the elevator to the Embassy lobby and walked past the Marine guards and stood looking down Embassy Row.

In other parts of San Nicolas, in any area except Embassy Row, William Keith Hall might have been mistaken for a native Costa Verdean. He was a fraction of an inch over six feet tall. He had dark thick hair, not like the blond hair of the usual North American or the brown or the red. The tan acquired during his four years in South America, the last year and a half in Costa Verde, was just the right tint. It seemed to point to Spanish blood, the aristocratic blend that was never more than one-eighth native stock and the rest that of the Spanish colonists that ruled Costa Verde until the waves of revolution swept through South

America. The nose was right also. It was narrow and the bone was like a knife blade.

The language school at the Company's farm in Virginia had given him a good base. Now he spoke almost flawless Spanish with the dips and turns and the slang that stamped it as Costa Verdean. His eyes were as dark as the lumps of coal still buried a mile deep in the mine.

He stood on the sidewalk that ran down Embassy Row and had his slow, long look in both directions. It was approaching noon, the rest and lunch time, and he saw few Costa Verdeans. That was as he wanted it. He stepped down from the curb and crossed the wide avenue and entered the new arcade of shops that had been built in the last year to accomodate the needs of the Embassy Row staffs. The arcade was a maze and tangle of clothing shops and wine stores, jewelry stalls and specialty food markets.

The first shop to the right, after he entered, sold wine. The owner, a dry little man in a gray business suit, recognized Hall because of the expensive purchases he had made over the last year. He smiled and nodded and left Hall to browse among the tilted racks. Five minutes passed. Hall moved from rack to rack, reading a label here and there. His eyes reached beyond the wine bottles. He watched the arcade entrance. Another five minutes passed. When Hall was ninety percent certain that he was not being followed, he selected two bottles of 1977 white Bordeaux and carried them to the counter. After he paid, and the bottles were wrapped, Hall scrawled his name on the parcel. He asked the owner to hold the wine for him until he had made other purchases in the far end of the arcade. The owner said that it would please him to serve the gentleman in any way that he could.

After a slow walk through the arcade, Hall left by the far entrance that led to the Plaza. A battered Ford taxi was at the curb. Will entered it and gave the driver an address on the Avenue Boliver. It was a part of town Hall knew well. On the north side of that block of Boliver were the small inexpensive cafes where the workers and the tradespeople had their lunches. On the south side of that same block was the Union Nationale cooperative store, an American-style department center for members of the union and their families.

It was a short ride. Will left the taxi and stood in front of one of the cafes until he was sure that the taxi had gone a distance and had been swallowed up in the rush of noon traffic. He found a slot in the traffic and crossed the Avenue to the Union Nationale store. He entered and passed through a men's clothing section and a boot shop. There was an elevator at the rear of the first floor. When the doors opened, he entered it and rode it to the first stop, the second floor. Only a woman and two children exited with him. He stopped long enough to see the woman and the children enter a children's clothing area. Then he located the down stairs. He pushed through the door and stood there for a count of sixty. Satisfied, he walked down the stairs to the first floor and found the exit to his left. That exit led to an alley lined with trash barrels and waste receptacles. Beyond that alley, seventy-five yards away, he could see the buildings on the Avenue San Martin.

He checked his watch as he walked down the alley. Almost noon. On time or about on time. Usually Paul Marcos left his office a few minutes after twelve and ate in a small café around the corner. Hall reached the mouth of the alley and waited. He was on the north side of San Martin. Almost directly across the Avenue, at a right angle, was the old gray building that housed the offices of the moderate party. A single white door without glass led to four steps. Wrought iron railings bordered the steps.

One minute passed. Then five. Just when Hall was about to decide that he'd missed Marcos the white door opened and Paul stood in the doorway. A tall thin man in his late forties, with the paler tint of the aristocrat. Graying hair cut short. A pencil line of a mustache on his upper lip. He held a white hat in one hand.

Will Hall pushed away from the alley wall. He took one step. At that moment, Paul turned aside and allowed a young woman to step through the doorway ahead of him. It wasn't a girl Hall knew and he hesitated and backed away. He was undecided, not sure that he could approach Paul while he was accompanied by someone he didn't know. Across the street, Paul took the girl's arm and they started down the stairs. Hall decided that he would have to take the risk. He stepped away from the alley and moved toward the curb. He stopped there and lifted an arm, about to wave toward Paul and try to get his attention.

That was when the first shot was fired.

The first round struck Paul in the chest and slammed him back against the closed door. He sat there, stunned, his hands coming up slowly and clasping across his chest. The girl with Paul turned and screamed.

Then the second shot was fired. It was so close that it could have been an echo of the first shot. This time a part of Paul's chin disappeared and a huge hole appeared in his throat.

A third shot struck the girl in the back as she leaned down toward Paul. It was like a fist rammed her in the back and tumbled her across Paul.

A squat dark man in peasant clothing and wearing a stained white hat ran down the street from Hall's right and stopped on the bottom step and stared down at Paul and the girl.

A gawker, will Hall thought.

The dark man's hand went under his loose white shirt. There was a pistol in that hand when it cleared the shirt. The man stepped up two stairs and emptied the pistol into the two forms. The man turned and leaped down to the sidewalk. A dark sedan pulled level, the door on the curb side swung open, and the man with the pistol jumped headfirst into the back of the car. The sedan roared away in a cloud of black smoke.

Odd. The street was suddenly empty. Blood pooled under the two bodies. Yes, bodies, Will told himself. He knew there was nothing he could do for them. He backed into the alley and walked quickly to the doorway and entered the Union Nationale cooperative store.

Five minutes later he left the taxi at the Plaza side of the arcade. On his way through the arcade, he stopped at the wine shop and retrieved his parcel. He crossed to the American Embassy and entered past the Marine guards. He rode the elevator to the third floor. There had been no calls for him while he was gone. He sat behind his desk and waited. He knew the phone would ring within the hour.

The call from Valdez came twenty minutes later.

On the drive to the apartment Valdez kept in the city, Hall turned on the car radio and listened to the state-owned and controlled news. News interrupted music about every five minutes. Paul Marcos and a secretary who worked at the moderate party headquarters had been murdered by suspected elements of the leftist rebel forces. That and little else. The government had ordered a state funeral for Senor Marcos and there would be other honors as well.

The apartment house was guarded by soldiers of the Republic. Four outside on the street, two in the lobby and two more in the hallway outside the penthouse apartment where Valdez lived. Hall was passed from guard unit to guard unit and, after a final search and frisk, he was allowed to enter the apartment where Valdez waited for him.

There was indio blood in Valdez. All of it was indio, Hall thought. The dark skin and the flat forehead. And, as it was with some of them, the cunning and the incredible streak of cruelty. He had started as a soldier in the province army and he had worked his way into the state secret police. With a special determination, and a cruelty that fascinated those around him, he had moved beyond the military into a position as the private security chief for the mining interests in the northern province. Now, in the struggle for control of his country, he spoke for the right-wing interests. He was a front man. A native who stood in for the secretive people, the U.S. mining interests and the rich aristocrats.

Will Hall had seen pictures of him taken ten years ago. He'd been a strong man then, with the shoulders of a peasant worker and the body of a wrestler. Soft living had put weight on him and inactivity, sloth, had turned that weight into layers and layers of fat.

"A drink, Mr. Hall?"

"Gin and tonic."

While Valdez mixed the drink, Hall looked around the large living room. It was decorated with the best of the native art, wood and stone carvings, and the walls were draped with the finest native weaving. The total effect was that of money and taste. But the room said nothing about Valdez. Whips and racks and razor blades and knives, that was the real Valdez. He moved well for a man his size. Valdez crossed to Hall and handed him the gin and tonic. "You Americans act rapidly," he said.

They were speaking English. It was a choice Valdez made. He was proud, he said, of his "gift of tongues." It was, Hall thought, a limited gift and he was not certain what Valdez meant.

Hall looked at his watch. "I'm on time."

"No, no." Valdez's huge body shook with laughter. "I meant the other matter." Valdez sat heavily on the sofa and lifted his large stem glass of red wine. His eyes closed and he smiled. "But we will pretend it is what I meant. I will compliment you on your promptness."

Hall knew better than to push at Valdez. The indio cunning would see through him. He took the chair Valdez indicated and sipped his drink and let the huge man tell him what the purpose of the meeting was.

An unwilling informant had told Valdez that a shipment of Cuban weapons was expected by the rebels within the next week. Valdez had heard of the marvels of the Company's spy in the sky, the satellite orbit. Would it be possible for the spy in the sky to locate the mother ship as it approached the coast of Costa Verde? Would it be possible for him to be warned when the offloading took place?

Hall said he would pass on the request to the Company in Washington.

He finished his drink. Valdez led him to the door. He was laughing again. "Such promptitude," Valdez said. Still laughing, he closed the door behind Hall.

Near the elevator, the two guards held and fondled a frightened young girl. The girl wore the uniform of a cleaning woman. Tearful as the girl was, she did not cry out or protest. Her eyes begged for help from Hall. He looked away and got into the elevator when it reached the floor. Riding down to the lobby, he told himself once again that this was the way Costa Verde was and would always be. The animals ran the country. Especially now that Paul Marcos was dead.

It was a hunch, a guess on his part.

His Company credentials got him past the gate of the military air base to the north of the city. His name was on the authorized list kept in the guard booth. After he entered, he drove along the road that led to the control tower. Finally, when he was near it, he avoided the V.I.P. parking and took a left turn and parked in the lot a distance away. He parked with the nose of the car forward, facing the runway. From there he could see the executive Lear jet that had been towed into position in the shade of the tower. The pilot was already at the controls, doing his checkout of the engines and the instruments.

Along the side of the Lear was the logo and the bold lettering:
United Mining, Ltd.

Hall didn't have long to wait. What they called a "mule", a tow tractor that was used to pull aircraft around the parking areas and the hangers, rumbled around the side of the tower and braked beside the Lear. The driver wore the green coveralls of an airport crewman. Two men sat in the back of the "mule". Even before they left the tractor, Hall knew who they were. He recognized the flat elongated face of Stoddard and beside him, on his left, the round Irish face of Higgins. It was The Team. What they joked about around the Company as The Bug Squad.

Stoddard was out of the "mule" first. He whipped one leg over the side of the tractor and stepped away. Higgins was next, slower, limping on what appeared to be a bruised right leg. Both men moved to the back of the "mule" and lifted a shiny, metallic footlocker from the back seat. They carried it, sharing the weight of it, to the door of the Lear. The footlocker was heavy and the strain showed in the faces of the two men. Good reason why it should be, Hall knew. It probably had enough armaments and weapons in it to start a small war.

Foolishness. Later he would tell himself it was foolishness and pride and anger. Hall opened the door of the car and stepped out. There was a raised concrete barrier in front of the car and he stepped forward and stood on it and stared at the two men.

Higgins saw him first. They had turned the footlocker, narrow side first, and pushed it into the Lear. Higgins backed away and turned to wave at the driver of the tow tractor. The hand stopped halfway to his shoulder when he saw Hall. Higgins reached behind him and touched Stoddard on the back. His lips moved but Hall did not know what he said.

Stoddard did a slow spin and faced the parking lot. His face was like gray stone. The narrow mouth was like a knife slash. Then the lips curled into a smile. Stoddard did a slow bow, almost like a performer. When he straightened up, he nodded at Higgins and they boarded the plane and closed the cabin door behind them. A couple of minutes later, the wheel chocks were pulled and the Lear taxied away from the tower and headed for one of the runways.

Hall remained where he was until the Lear was a tiny speck in the sky.

Two days later Frank Springs was ordered in from El Salvador to replace Will Hall. Within a matter of hours, Hall was on a commercial jet headed north to Washington.

CHAPTER TWO

He brooded from a distance, away from Washington and the Company. His resignation was written on his first day back and accepted, he thought, with too much pleasure by the Director. Afterall, the thinking went, Hall had been wrong about the situation in Costa Verde and he had let his feelings get in the way of what the Company and the United States wanted. It did not matter what Hall thought about the way they had gone around him for the hit on Paul Marcos. And it did not matter that he felt wronged because they had run a dirty operation in his backyard without informing him about it.

"An executive decision," the Assistant Director said.

Executive decision was as exact as it ever got. It could mean the President had given his okay. Or it could have been decided at a lower rung, perhaps by someone at the South American desk.

So, Hall brooded at a distance. North Carolina seemed far enough away. He had his back pay, and a token severance from the Company and there was the trust fund he hadn't touched during his years with the government. An inheritance from his mother. It was enough to live on comfortably for ten or fifteen years if he never worked at all.

His mother had been a Harker, one of the big tobacco families in Winston-Salem. Not close enough to the center of the Harker money for the inheritance to be worth millions but there was enough stock to matter when the cancer scare came and Harker Tobacco diversified. Harker investments in fast food and drugs and soft drinks prospered. By the time Hall's mother died, the stock was worth four times what it had been worth when the sole products of Harker were four kinds of cigarettes and two kinds of plug chewing tobacco.

And Hall owned the house in Blowing Rock. It was really a summer mountain cottage. The walls were fitted stone and there was a wide porch that looked over a straight drop of thousands of feet. At the bottom was the Gap. On the other side of the Gap was Grandfather Mountain.

Hall remembered beautiful summers spent there, peaceful weeks as a boy when he and his mother and an aunt lived in the house and his father, working in Winston-Salem, came to join them on the weekends.

After the house was cleaned and a crew of carpenters weatherproofed it, Will Hall moved in. It was December and there was snow and the air was clean and brisk. Hall spent his days reading and watching television. On the weekends, if the highways were clear, he drove his old black BMW in one direction or the other. Toward Raleigh or Durham and, at times, to Chapel Hill. Each was a different kind of weekend. He'd stay at a hotel or a motel. The days were for aimless wandering. At night he went looking for music. Country and western at a road-house near Raleigh, a string quartet at Duke and rock and roll at the Cat's Cradle in Chapel Hill.

And all that time, he watched the news from Costa Verde. It was no surprise to him, in January, two weeks before the election, that Valdez and his goon squads broke the moderate faction and jailed the leaders. The left wing, the rebels, was smashed in a massive army sweep through the northern provinces. There was no quarter given. Rebels who surrendered were executed on the spot.

The President of Costa Verde declared a state of emergency and suspended the elections, he said, until a calm and peace returned to his country.

It would never happen, Hall knew.

The state-sanctioned murder squads swept through the midnight and pre-dawn streets of the cities. The victims were the supporters of the moderate and the left-wing causes. Whole families were murdered along roadsides or killed and tossed in trash dumps.

So much for the Company. So much for the choice the Company had made.

His tan faded in the winter sun.

No longer brooding. Instead, he remembered. His father had died his first year at Yale. His mother, who had been over-ruled by her husband when she wanted Will to attend Duke University, died during his final semester. He'd been rootless, at odds with himself. He had thought that the natural extension of his education would be graduate work in history. It was for that reason he made an appointment with Professor Charles Edward Rockwall. Over tea, alone in one end of the huge College lounge, Rockwall gave Hall no chance to ask his question about graduate study and a life in teaching.

"I have had my eye on you from the beginning," he told Hall. And then he talked of his generation's secret war, vague tales of his World War Two experiences in the O.S.S. "Wild Bill" Donavan and Allan Dulles and the old boy network of gentlemen who fought that improbable war and won their share of it.

"Our class has an obligation," Rockwall told Hall. "And a destiny that lesser men cannot imagine in their wildest dreams."

Two days after graduation, Hall met with the Assistant Director in an unmarked office near the Green in downtown New Haven. The interview seemed unstructured, casual, but Will Hall knew better. It was a masterful probe and counter-probe of his mind and his instincts.

Later that month, while his former classmates toured Europe or vacationed at the beach or in the mountains, Hall underwent basic training at Fort Jackson. His record was specially coded. After completion of basic training, he was transferred to Fort Bragg for paratrooper instruction. A day before the ceremony to receive his jump badge, he was taken from the barracks late at night and flown to the Farm in Virginia. His service record and all evidence of his existence as a solder disappeared.

He became a shadow figure.

"Our class has an obligation." He remembered Rockwall's words during the long months of training at the Farm. Weapons, explosives, communication, languages and political realism for underdeveloped countries.

He kept his faith, his high idealism in the face of the pragmatics of political warfare. He continued to believe all through his posting to Brazil and Chile, right up to his last year and a half in Costa Verde. Until that moment, near high noon, in San Nicolas when Paul Marcos died.

Now, on the mountain, wandering the windy roads, he could no longer hear the exact tone Professor Rockwall had used. Was there humor there now? A whisper of cynicism?

Rockwall's words rolled in his mind a hundred ways. Until he no longer knew the proper inflection. Only Rockwall might have helped him. That was, however, no longer possible. Professor Rockwell had died of lung cancer in the Yale Medical Center during the first month of Hall's posting to Costa Verde.

Then it was February. A snowstorm dumped four inches on Blowing Rock. The last flakes were felling when Hall left his warm bed and added a split log to the banked coals in the fireplace grate. He made a pot of coffee in the kitchen and, bundled against the cold, he carried his mug to the wide porch and sat in one of the rockers and watched the last of the snow fall between him and the mountain across the Gap. It was restful, it was peaceful and so beautiful that he felt the changes in himself

Washington and the power struggles, the backbiting and the betrayals, all seemed a million miles away. A speck of dust in the sea. It was done. The bitterness and the anger so shrunken and dried inside him that he could no longer find it.

When the snow fall ended, he had breakfast and sat before the roaring fire and read Babel's *Red Cavalry Tales*. He was still reading, and watching a new log catch fire, when he heard the three short beeps from the mail jeep horn. It was the driver's way of telling him that he'd arrived. Hall put the book aside, pulled on some heavy boots and slogged through the snow to the mail box at the end of the driveway.

The usual pitiful collection of mail. A bank statement. A real estate brochure. Announcement of a sale at The Hub, a men's shop in Chapel Hill. Finally, a letter. He stopped, huddled over against the wind and opened it. Not a letter. A note, from Denise Lawton, a girl in graduate school at The University of North Carolina, inviting him to a party at her house this coming Saturday. He'd met her at the Cat's Cradle one night and spent the weekend with her. It had been a fun weekend, dancing to a new wave band at the Cradle, having dinner at a vegetarian restaurant she liked, walks around the campus, and best of all waking in the morning in her bed. That part surprised him, how much he liked the girl, and he had pulled back later. It was a lonely time for him and he didn't want to over-estimate the emotions of a single weekend spent with a girl he hardly knew. Almost a month had passed. He hadn't called her. The *please call me if you can come* and the single exclamation mark seemed almost pathetic.

He continued his walk up the driveway. There was a magazine wrapped in a wide band of brown paper. And that was it. Inside the house, he tossed the unopened bank statement on the kitchen table. He knew there was still a healthy balance and it was too early to check it against his check book. Later. After he refilled his coffee mug, he looked at the note from Denise Lawton again. He was tempted. He wanted to see her again. Still, it was only Tuesday. He'd wait another day before he decided.

The magazine. He slipped the paper wrapper aside and unfolded the magazine. *The Truth Seeker*.

It wasn't his usual reading matter. And he'd certainly never subscribed. He reached into the trashcan and retrieved the mailing wrapper. There was no mistake. His name and address. Hand written. Odd.

He had never read *The Truth Seeker*, but he did know what it was. The magazine was a holdover from the Civil Rights and Anti-war movements. Around the Company, the hard liners considered the journal subversive. One of their last in-country illegal operations had been an attempt to close the magazine down. First they'd tried to attack the financing. It had been a failure. One of the big backers was a little old lady in New York whose background was spotless. Flora Tucker had opened her purse to *The Truth Seeker* when her favorite grandson died in a rice paddy in Vietnam. Her influence reached all the way to the White House. The Company backed away from her. The attack shifted toward the staff, the usual blackmail and slander approach. The editor, Enos Blackman, hadn't fallen for any of the honey traps. Not for the pretty boys or the women. In fact, he'd laughed at it all, as if he'd known what was going on the whole time.

The Company had to pull back before they'd settled upon the third phase of the attack. The Director of the F.B.I. caught wind of the operation and railed at the Company. In-country was the territory of the F.B.I and he was jealous and protective. He would not stand for meddling, even if it meant he had to go to the President.

So, the Company got a black eye and little to show for an expensive undertaking.

Hall carried the magazine into the living room. He put Babel aside and read the first article. It was a long, detailed account of the circumstances surrounding the right-wing coup in Chile.

THE SPY IN A BOX

Most of the material was correct, though the writer missed some of the Company's involvement in several key events. After he finished the article, he thumbed through the rest of the contents. An article on Cuban intervention in Africa. An article on the American efforts and counter-moves against Cuban influence.

On the back, inside cover there was a listing of articles to be published in the March issue. Hall's heart thudded, stopped and then started again.

It was there, heading the list.

William K. Hall, ex-Company field man, tells the truth about U.S. intervention in Costa Verdean political affairs and the untold story of the murder of Paul Marcos.

Hall dropped the magazine on the floor and walked into the kitchen. He took down the bottle of black Jack Daniels and poured a stiff drink. Carrying the drink with him into the bedroom he packed an overnight bag. Then he sat on the bed and called the Winston-Salem airport. There was snow on the runways and no flights until the next morning. He booked the first flight leaving for New York.

He had a restless night, a night when he drank too much.

By nine the next morning, he was on the ground at LaGuardia and in a taxi headed for the city.

At first, he thought of the Village as an unlikely location for the offices of a publication. On the other hand, consider the publication, he told himself. But that wasn't fair. Another magazine, after it achieved some success and solid financial backing, might have moved into a better suite of offices, to a better address. Not *The Truth Seeker*. For its thirty years of publication, the same Sheridan Square address remained on the cover.

Will Hall climbed the narrow flight of stairs that ran between a deli and a bar. The editorial offices were to the right, above the bar. The door to the outer offices was unlocked. Hall entered and stood at a chest high counter. Beyond the counter were three desks. There was a hand bell on the counter. Hall waited. After a couple of minutes, an incredibly pencil thin girl dressed in tan slacks and a bulky green sweater came from an office in the rear. She was munching a cookie. She stopped and brushed a few crumbs from her lips.

"I'd like to see Mr. Blackman."

"He's busy at the moment. If you …"

"Tell him it's William Hall."

For an instant he had the feeling she was going to jam the rest of her cookie into her mouth and leap the counter and hug him. She quivered and took a deep breath. "Of course, he'll want to see you."

Enos Blackman. On the flight from Winston-Salem Hall remembered some of the dossier the Company had on file. Fought in World War Two. Three battle stars, two Purple Hearts, recommended for the Medal of Honor. Probably not awarded, though deserved, because it was near the end of the war. Returned to the States after the war with the idea of writing a novel. A summary of the novel, from an editor who rejected the book at Random House, began with the statement that the whole concept of Blackman's novel was banal. That it was an allegory of Christ at the Battle of the Bulge. When the book found no publisher, Blackman clerked for a time for a bookshop in the Village. When the Korean War began, Blackman started *The Truth Seeker* on his savings. It was more a broadsheet than a journal at the time. Blackman argued against the Korean war from beginning to end as a battle to stop true determinism, the United States on the side of repression and dictatorship.

When the Korean War ended, the magazine floundered for a long time, searching for a new issue. He found that cause in the Civil Rights upheavals of the early 1960's. He marched in

Alabama and Mississippi, a bear of a man who carried an old Army Colt .45 under his dirty raincoat. Once, when a Klan member tried to intimidate him, he pushed the raincoat open and showed the butt of the .45 and said, "I am not necessarily non-violent myself. You try me."

With the bad years behind them, the rough times, the magazine found plenty of backing during the Vietnam War. Still, from all appearances, Enos Blackman had not changed his style of living. He still looked as if he dressed from the rack at a local discount department store and he lived in a set of small rooms around the corner on Christopher Street.

"Come in, Mr. Hall." Enos Blackman was a thick tree trunk of a man, clean shaved, with a bald pate and the hairiest arms Hall had ever seen.

"You know me?" Hall took the chair across the desk from Blackman.

"Through letters and our telephone conversations."

"I'm not sure I'm the William K. Hall you think I am."

Blackman stared at Hall. Then he shook his head slowly from side-to-side. "Stella, bring me the picture."

The thin girl entered the office a minute later and dropped a glossy on Blackman's desk. Before she left, she smiled at Hall. Blackman turned the photograph toward Hall.

Someone, perhaps a photo editor, had marked the picture with a grease pencil, narrowing the photograph until it was a bust shot of Hall. From what Hall could see outside the markings, the photograph had been taken in a bookstore. The Intimate in Chapel Hill, Hall thought. He couldn't, for the life of him, remember when the picture was taken.

Hall pushed the glossy away. "That's me."

"What is the problem, Mr. Hall?"

"I didn't write the article."

Blackman seemed puzzled. "Then you are a different William Keith Hall? Hall is a common name."

Hall shook his head. "I'm the right William Hall. I was with the Company in South American. My last station there was Costa Verde."

"You're going to have to spell this out for me."

"I know nothing about this article."

"I see." Enos Blackman lifted a heavy hand and rubbed his eyes. "You've changed your mind about the article? You don't want it published now?" Blackman lowered the hand and looked at Hall with red-rimmed, tired eyes. "We talked about this. I said they'd try to pressure you."

"I've had no pressure."

"I told you it wouldn't be easy." Blackman continued as if he hadn't heard Hall. "I warned you that your convictions would have to be strong. I guess they weren't as strong as you believed they were." Blackman shook his head sadly at Hall. "Stella, has the check returned that we mailed Mr. Hall in North Carolina?"

"Two days ago," Stella said from beyond the doorway.

Blackman left the office. When he returned, he dropped a cancelled check on the desk in front of him. Hall lifted the check and turned it in his hands. It was in the amount of a thousand dollars and it had been deposited to his bank in Blowing Rock. The signature on the back of the check looked good enough to be his own.

Hall passed the check to Blackman. "Pretend I have amnesia. Tell me how it came about."

In late December, Blackman received a call, long distance, from North Carolina. The caller said that he was William K. Hall and that he wanted to offer *The Truth Seeker* an article on an important subject. Blackman was interested in the topic, the Company's involvement in the political affairs of Costa Verde. He told the caller as much. Then he was even more excited to learn that the caller identified himself as a former station man with the Company. The article arrived at the journal office a few days later. It was all the caller had promised that it would be. Since then, there had been several phone calls and letters. The phone calls were usually on the weekends. The biography and the photo arrived and the payment, higher than *The Truth Seeker* could usually afford, was mailed to the Banford Street address in Blowing Rock.

Blackman paused. He took a deep breath. "This is not a child's game, Mr. Hall. I bought the article and I paid for it. There is no way that publication can be stopped at this point in the process. And, right now, I'm not even sure that I would obey a court order."

Hall stood. "You've heard nothing from the federal government?"

"Nothing," Blackman said. "I guess they don't read *The Truth Seeker*"

"They read you," Hall said. "Don't doubt that for a minute. Did you send me the latest issue?"

"I thought you'd like to see the listing for your article," Blackman said.

Whoever built the frame probably hadn't realized that might happen or they were so confident of his fate that they simply didn't care if he was tipped off before publication.

Enos Blackman followed him into the outer office. He stood behind the counter until Hall reached the door that led to the hallway. "Where do we stand now, Mr. Hall?"

Hall paused at the door. "I'm the goat."

Late afternoon. It was snowing in New York. It was a fine powder like sand. Hall checked his small bag and his topcoat at the checkroom downstairs and climbed the stairs to the Four Seasons. He took a seat at the bar, near the stairs so that he could watch the arrivals. At the same time, by turning in his chair, he could watch the snow through what he considered some of the better windows in the world.

He drank dark rum over the rocks. The first fifteen minutes he sat at the bar no one entered that he knew. At five-thirty exactly a tall, handsome man stopped at the head of the steps and looked at Hall. Everything about him, the cut of the suit, the texture of the shirt and the knot in the tie spoke of money and success. Until he moved. Then he seemed to be an actor only wearing the clothing for an hour on a stage. That sense, the feeling that the garments did not like his body.

Ben Jacobi crossed to the bar and touched Hall on the shoulder before he took the empty stool on his right.

"It's been a long time," Ben said.

"Four years." Hall waited for Ben to order and he nodded at the check in front of him when the bartender brought Jacobi a J&B on the rocks. After the bartender moved away, Hall grinned at Ben. "If you're going to come in places like this you've got to stop drinking that lower-class scotch."

Jacobi poured back half the drink in one swallow. "It suits me." Then he laughed. "Speaking of suits, what you think of these threads?"

"Looks stolen to me, Hall."

"You're a great kidder, Hall." Jacobi rattled the ice in his glass. "I don't have much time. You said you wanted a favor."

"I might need a specialist."

Ben leaned toward Hall. "What kind?"

"B and E."

"What's wrong? Don't you boys do your own these days?"

"I'm not with them anymore," Hall said.

"That's a horse with a different stride."

Hall nodded. "I thought it might be."

"What kind of B and E?"

"A popcorn box. I need to get past a door and into a file cabinet or two."

Ben lowered his voice. "Any security?"

"None."

"Five bills will get you the best there is." Jacobi poked a finger into the gray silk of his tie. "Me."

"For a popcorn box?"

Ben shook his head. "For the fun of it."

Hall sipped his dark rum. "I've got a few things to do. I want it to hang fire for a week or so. Might be I won't need it."

"You call me. Twenty-four hours' notice, that's all it takes."

After Ben Jacobi left, Hall watched the sky grow dark. After a time, the powder snow looked like black sand.

The month's bill from Southern Bell was in the mail box beside the road. Hall stuffed the envelope in his topcoat pocket and parked the black BMW in the driveway. After he tossed the overnight bag on the bed, he got a fire going in the fireplace. Then he carried the envelope into the kitchen. He poured a Jack Daniels, had a sip, and opened the bill from Southern Bell. He knew what he'd find. In the list of toll calls three to the same New York number. From the dates, looking at the calendar, he realized the calls had been placed while he was out of town, on his weekend rambles. He put the phone bill aside and found the unopened bank statement he'd received the day before. He found the one thousand dollar deposit.

That was it. He was boxed. The problem was that he didn't know why and he didn't know who would go to all that trouble.

CHAPTER THREE

It rained early in the morning, sometime after midnight, and it was a soft, slow drumming on the tin roof. Will Hall heard it begin, his eyes closed tight against the darkness in the bedroom, and it should have lulled him to sleep. It didn't. His body was jumpy after the trip to New York. Also, there were questions that he couldn't answer and there was a jumble of ideas in his mind. The head of an idea chased the tail of another idea around and around. Until he said, "Sleep, dammit," and he blew a cold wind through his brain, ear-to-ear, and the rain lulled him into a peaceful darkness. A darkness where it didn't matter which was the head of an idea and which was the tail.

The next morning, he called Denise in Chapel Hill. He called early to catch her before she left for campus. He was, he told her, sorry it had taken him so long to reply to her note. There had been some business out of town and he hadn't known how long it would take to complete that. But it was done now and he could attend her party. In fact, he planned to spend the whole day in Chapel Hill. Maybe they could have a late lunch or an early dinner before the party? The offer seemed to please her and soften her. He said he would call her as soon as he reached town.

He placed the phone on the base and stared down at it. That ought to do it. Assuming the phone was tapped. And assuming there was another call that might need to be made. Another ribbon or bow that would add a flourish on the package they had made out of him.

THE SPY IN A BOX

Two days later, Saturday morning, he dressed in slacks, a sweater and a parka and carried a suit bag and a shaving kit to the BMW. It was ten o'clock exactly when he backed down the driveway and followed the twisting road down into Blowing Rock. He took the highway and followed it for several miles. Speeding up and slowing down, changing lanes, while he watched his rearview mirror. No one car caught his attention. Still, he knew it would be well done and even a trained man might have trouble selecting the follow car. Ten miles beyond Blowing Rock, he stopped at a service station for gas. While the attendant worked over the BMW, he entered the station and bought a pack of cigarettes from the machine. Then he stood at the window and watched the traffic.

If there was a tail, a single tail, the sudden stop was a crisis point. The man in a follow car would have to make a quick decision, whether to drive past the gas station and try to resume the tail down the highway a distance. Or he could stop for gas too.

As it happened, no car pulled into the station. That would have been asking too much. A look at the tail if there was one.

It was time for the risk. He knew this stretch of highway well. Two or three miles past the gas station, there was a crossover, a place where he could turn onto the dual lane headed back toward Blowing Rock, He made the turn. He watched his rear-view mirror. No car followed him.

He drove back through Blowing Rock. He followed the twisting road toward his house and reached the driveway and passed it. The next house was around a bend. The Winters cottage. He knew the Winters weren't using it. He pulled from the road and parked in the driveway. It took him almost twenty minutes to cross the rough landscape between the Winters house and the back of his house. He was perspiring and puffing when he climbed the back steps that led to his kitchen. He stood there for a time, getting his breath even, and listening for sounds in the house. The old flooring would creak under weight. Five minutes passed. He heard nothing inside the house. He entered and crossed through the kitchen. The living room was empty. He settled in for the wait.

There was a chill in the room. The log in the fireplace was down to coals. He drew the parka tight across him and shivered. On the arm of the stuffed chair was the only weapon in the house, an old .22 automatic that he'd found in the attic during the cleanup. He remembered the automatic from his childhood. He and his father had used it, some long summer ago, to shoot at cans from the porch. There were nine fresh rounds in the clip, from a box he'd bought in Winston-Salem on a shopping trip.

After about thirty minutes, the phone rang. He ignored it. Twelve rings before the caller gave up. That was part of a pattern, he knew, and he lifted the .22 automatic and jacked a round into the chamber. Safety off. He held the automatic with his finger outside the trigger guard.

He estimated the driving time from the center of Blowing Rock. Four or five minutes if the driver caught the lights. It was six minutes later by the wall clock when he heard the truck pull into his driveway. He crossed to the window. A blue van with HUNT BROTHERS PLUMBING painted on the side of it. He returned to his chair.

He felt the weight on the porch, the footsteps, and he guessed there was one man. A pause, a shifting of weight, and then hall heard the scrape of the key in the lock. Some show they'd put on for him, he thought. They had a key. No tiresome lock picking for them.

The door opened. Hall felt the rush of cold wind. A man in coveralls stood, backlighted for an instant, in the doorway. Then he stepped forward and closed the door behind him. The man carried a tool chest in one hand. With the other hand he groped for the light switch.

The bright overhead light flared. The man turned. When he saw Hall, he almost dropped the tool chest.

"Put it down easy, Freddy," Hall said.

Freddy Webb bent his knees and placed the tool chest on the floor directly in front of him.

"Hands clasped behind your head." Webb did as he was told. "Now, step away from the tool chest."

Webb stepped over the chest, two paces and he stopped. Hall wagged the .22 automatic at him. "Over there." Hall stood. 'Turn around, Freddy." When the man's back was to him Hall patted down, neck to shoe tops. Nothing. No weapons, not even a pocket knife.

Hall backed away, "Face me. With your hands where they are, sit down and cross your legs in front of you."

Freddy sat down heavily, off balance. Hall thought it might be a try of some kind but Freddy righted himself. When his legs were crossed in front of him, Hall circled him and lifted the tool chest. He carried it to the stuffed chair and sat down. With his free hand, Hall flipped the catches on the chest and opened it. It looked real enough. An assortment of tools. Off to one side something wrapped in a clean red rag. Hall pulled the cloth away. He dropped the rag and picked up the .357 Python with a two-inch barrel. He placed the .357 next to his leg, between his thigh and the chair.

"Long time no see, Freddy."

"I've been wondering why you call me Freddy. I don't know you, mister."

"Sure, you do." Hall closed the chest. "Quick entry used to be your specialty. You still working for the same shop?"

"Smart mouth," Freddy said.

"I think you owe me fifty or sixty dollars for some phone calls."

"I don't know anything about any phone calls."

"What's the plot for today? Another call to Enos Blackman?"

"You better talk to the Director," Freddy said.

"I thought you heard. I'm retired."

"Nobody retires."

"I did," Hall said.

"The Director will want to talk to you."

"This is some gold watch you boys are putting together for me."

"You keep messing and it'll be a dum-dum behind your ear."

"Threats, Freddy?" Hall smiled. "Tell me about the phone calls."

"I don't know…"

Hall fired a shot with the .22 a fraction of an inch past Freddy's left ear. Wood splinters flew from a panel in the door.

"That's to get your attention. The next one is for your kneecap. You'll remember me the rest of your life, every time you limp."

"Alright." Perspiration matted Freddy's face, even in the chill of the room. "I'm supposed to plant some bugs. They're in the chest."

"Why?"

"You ask why? After what you've done?"

"What have I done?"

"Sold out the Company," Freddy said.

Hall leaned forward and opened the chest. He poked around in the mass of tools until he found the bugs. He tossed the package into the fireplace.

"I think I wet myself," Freddy said.

"It's a rough life."

"You ain't seen rough yet." Freddy looked down at the crotch of his coveralls. A wet stain was spreading there.

"And you haven't made any phone calls here?"

"From here?" Freddy shook his head.

"Your first visit?"

Webb nodded.

"The key?"

Webb understood the rest of the question. "Before you turned, while you were still with the Company, you rented out the place during the summers. Some realtor here in town handled it for you. There used to be a spare key on the pegboard in their office."

"You get it there?" Hall stepped over the tool chest and squatted beside the fireplace. He stacked kindling over the ashes and shoved in several wads of newspaper. He touched his lighter to the newsprint and, when it was burning, he backed away.

"No, I got it from the Warden."

Moss, the one they called the Warden, was in charge of internal security at the Company. He kept his eyes on all matters that involved agents, from their bank accounts to their bedroom lives.

The kindling caught. Hall added a split log and moved back to his chair. "Who's the Warden's second now?"

"Rivers."

Hall nodded. It sounded right. From the moment he recognized Freddy Webb, he'd known the phone calls to New York, the rigging of the thousand-dollar check, the whole box, were beyond a B and E man. It was the kind of work, however, that a man like Rivers might have relished. All matters sly and underhanded, those were in Rivers' ballpark.

Webb worked his shoulders. His arms were getting tired and cramping. He groaned. "The Director will want to see you."

"I'd rather see Rivers."

"That shouldn't be hard for a smart man like you." Another groan. "You going to keep me like this all day?"

Over the smell of the kindling and the oak, there was the scent of burning plastic and wiring. Freddy Webb looked in the direction of the fireplace. The electronic bugs were melting.

"There a tap on my phone?"

Webb nodded.

"Where?"

"You know Ma Bell loves us. The Warden figured you'd find any bug on the phone or in it."

"The same with any bugs here in the house?"

"That's right," Webb said. "The Warden wanted you lazy and sure of yourself before I dropped by."

True. It was a good assumption on the Warden's part. A week or ten days before, Hall had given up sweeping the house for bugs. It hadn't seemed worth the effort. Until now.

"I go now?" Webb jerked his head toward the fireplace when one of the bugs popped.

Hall nodded. "I appreciate you stopping by."

Webb used one hand to push himself to his feet. The other hand remained behind his head. When he was on his feet, he rubbed the muscles in his back. Then the free hand joined the other at his neck. "The tool chest? The piece?"

"The next time you drop by," Hall said.

"There won't be any next time."

"Too bad. It gets lonely up here."

Hall followed him to the door. He kept his distance while Webb opened the door and stepped onto the porch. When Webb reached the steps, Hall moved into the doorway. He stood there until Webb got into the van, turned it and headed for the road. He watched the driveway for ten minutes. Then he returned to the living room. He opened the phone book on the telephone table and found the emergency numbers. He dialed the fire station.

A woman answered. "Fire station."

"I want to talk to you, Rivers."

"What? You must have a wrong..."

"I said I want to talk to you, Rivers."

Hall placed the receiver on the base. He entered the kitchen and mixed himself a watered-down Jack Daniels. He returned to the living room and watched the fire. The smell of burning plastic and wiring was gone. He took his time with the drink. He'd just had the last swallow when the phone rang.

Hall lifted the receiver. He waited.

"I thought you were going to a party."

"That's what Webb thought too."

"Tricky of you," Rivers said. The voice was vaguely Harvard. Edged with upper class snot.

"You change Webb's diapers yet?"

"Did he have an accident?" Rivers laughed but there wasn't a pinch of amusement in the laughter. "The poor baby must have been nervous." There was a pause. "You really should go to the party."

"What's the point now?"

"I'm a guest there myself," Rivers said.

"I see." Hall let out a long breath. It was almost a whisper. "Maybe you could do me a favor."

"I might."

"Tell Denise I won't be there for the late lunch or early dinner."

"She already knows that," Rivers said. He broke the connection.

CHAPTER FOUR

The house was on Cameron Avenue, past the Carolina Inn and the frat houses and courts. It was wood frame, painted white, and the porch ran the length of the front of it and down the left side as well. The porch lights were on and as Hall drove past, he saw a couple mount the stairs and head for the front door.

Hall drove past once. Down the street a distance, he turned around in a driveway. He'd seen nothing out of the ordinary the first time by. The problem was that he wasn't certain what to look for. He didn't know what to expect. Somewhere, knowing that, Rivers was having his laugh.

Hall parked in a place on the street about half a block from the house. The Python .357 was in his parka pocket.

Wherever Rivers went there was security. There was no way he'd still have the Python on him when he met with Rivers. He looked around the car. There was a plastic litter bag hanging from the dashboard. Half full, cigarette packages, candy wrappers and kleenexes. He shoved the Python into the litter bag and molded the trash around the shape.

It was his second visit to the house. Denise shared it with two other girls. The other time he'd been there, the whole house smelled of perfume and talc. That followed the meeting with Denise at the Cat's Cradle when he'd picked her up. Or had it been the other way around? He wasn't certain now. Bed and breakfast with Denise. The time in bed had been strangely awkward, as if Denise's experience to this point had been a kind of instruction by the numbers. Breakfast, that Sunday morning,

THE SPY IN A BOX

had been relaxed, fun and talk. Three young girls and their sleep over boyfriends.

Hall stopped on the bottom step. Wryly, he wondered what sort of report Denise had turned in on him. Good in bed? Kinky? And he tried to remember what they'd talked about. The research she was doing that would lead to her dissertation? His fabricated tale of his life and what he was doing now? Or what he wasn't doing now?

Denise was near the front door when he entered and stopped in the hallway. She was slim and dark-haired, high-rumped with breasts that were too large for the rest of her body. Tonight she wore a long evening gown, green as bottle glass, and high necked, almost to her chin. Overdressed, he thought, or it could be a way of telling people that she knew what was proper even if they didn't.

When Denise saw him, she rushed through a crowd to reach him. While she hugged him, her hands moved down him, from his shoulders to his waist. From a distance it probably looked warm and friendly. Hall knew it for what it was. A competent frisk. All she left out was a kick to both legs to see if there was anything strapped to his calves.

"I'm glad you could come," Denise said.

"Wouldn't miss it for anything." Hall looked past her. He didn't see Rivers. "Anybody I know here?"

"A friend of a friend." Denise leaned close to him, as if to say something secret and tender. "He's in the upstairs bedroom."

"Yours?"

A nod. "You remember which one that was, don't you?"

He stepped around her. There was a cluster of graduate students at the bottom of the stairs. In the group, he recognized one of Denise's housemates, a doll-like blonde girl who was in English. He dipped his head toward her and smiled. With a mumbled "excuse me" he threaded his way through the group and climbed four steps before he turned. It wasn't like Rivers to be alone. When he travelled, there was usually a driver and a backup man. He didn't think Denise counted as either.

Then, in the corner of one eye, he saw the first one. He was trying to blend in, hoping to be taken as either an older graduate student or a professor who'd been invited because he was a good guy. A pale man in a Harris tweed jacket and a red knit tie. Now he was hunched over a book, one elbow hooked on the top of a tall bookcase. Hall remembered him from the Farm, the training ground for field men. The name slipped Hall but he recalled the man had taught silent killing. Hall put a hand on the bannister and waited. The man lifted his eyes from the book page and Hall winked at him before he turned and climbed the remainder of the staircase that led to the second floor.

So? Unless Rivers had changed his pattern, that left the driver. It was possible that Hall was going to see Rivers alone. Or had it been planned that way so that Hall would make that assumption? Perhaps.

The door to Denise's bedroom was at the near end of the hallway. The first door to the right. Hall stopped in front of the door and knocked. Once, twice.

The voice was muffled. "Come in, Hall."

Hall opened the door. He gave it a push and stood there, getting a full, long look at the room.

"Come in, Hall. We are alone."

"I had my doubts." Hall entered and closed the door behind him with a push. It was warm in the room and there were warring smells, perfume and talc and the harshness of the John Cotton's Mixture that Rivers smoked in his pipe. Hall took off his parka and dropped it on a chair.

Rivers sat on the edge of Denise's bed. He was partially dressed, wearing silk underwear, calf length socks and a blue quilted winter bathrobe. Rivers was around fifty and his hair had been gray since he was thirty. His eyes were a hard ice blue and he wore the neat, narrow mustache that was like a relic from the past. His hands were pale and lean and girl-like.

"You're early or I'm late," Rivers said.

"It might be a little of both. I don't think a time was set."

"One moment, please." River went into the bathroom. When he returned a minute later, he was wearing heavy tan twill trousers. "Do you think these are casual enough for this sort of gathering?"

"Probably."

Rivers sat in a low chair beside the bed and slipped his feet into black tassel loafers.

"How does Denise fit into this?" Hall said.

"A niece of mine." Rivers laughed. "She's one of our political study girls. Russian and Russian history. It just happened she was enrolled here when you moved back to North Carolina. When it turned out you spend a weekend here now and then, and that you liked decadent rock-and-roll, it was simple enough to set up a meeting between the two of you."

"Why go to the trouble?"

"We thought you might invite her to your house in Blowing Rock."

"Not likely," Hall said.

"She thought she was making progress."

"A beginner." Hall kept it hard, with an edge. "She'll never bait a decent honeytrap."

Rivers shook his head, a mock sadness on his face. "I'll tell her. She'll be disappointed."

"She knows. Women always know."

Rivers untied his robe and dropped it at the foot of the bed. He shook out a white broadcloth shirt and put it on quickly, as if ashamed to let Hall see his narrow chest and thin arms. Pale fingers worried at the buttons. "You, my friend," he said, "are in white water without a paddle."

"Part of that might be true. I am not, however, your friend."

"The rules are cut in stone and mounted on the mountain. That is the contract you signed. There was, you agreed, to be no publication without a prior review of the writing by the Director and the Assistant Director."

"I kept my bargain."

Rivers worked a tie under the collar of his shirt and began to tie a half Windsor. The tie was heavy tweed. His back was to Hall but he watched Hall in the mirror. "I am not sure I understand."

"I've been jobbed. I thought you did it."

"Tell me about it," Rivers said.

At the end of it, the recital of the facts by Hall, Rivers was dressed and ready for the party. He'd put on a stiff Irish tweed jacket and he'd brushed his gray hair with care and precision. He dropped his silver-backed hairbrush on the dressing table.

"It sounds like a cookie jar story to me." He mimicked a child's plaintive voice. "I didn't touch the cookie jar, mommy. It fell off the shelf and I caught it so it wouldn't break."

"What's my motive?"

"Disenchantment. The usual. A misdirected vision of what is good for our country.

Hall shook his head. "I'm out of it and good riddance to it. But I've got to admit it's a good box somebody built around me."

"I've seen the piece." Rivers smiled. "We have our ways as you well know. It's all there. The inside details you know from your time in Costa Verde. And one new fact. That snipers fired the first shots into Marcos and the girl. That the Team was in Costa Verde."

"Anybody with access to the file knows what I know."

"The thousand dollars?"

"Tell me where you bank and I'll deposit a thousand dollars into your account."

"The phone calls to Enos Blackman."

"All made on my phone on weekends, while I was away from Blowing Rock."

"Photographs of you entering and leaving Blackman's offices on Sheridan Square."

"Are they dated? Blackman says he only knows me from letters and phone calls."

"All of it fits," Rivers said.

"It should. It's tailored."

Rivers closed his eyes and shook his head. "I'll have to talk to the Director."

Hall picked up his parka. "In that case, I'll have a drink with the hostess and go home and wait to hear from you."

"One more matter. You have a weapon belonging to Webb."

Hall smiled. "It fell off a shelf and I caught it to keep it from breaking."

"I never liked you," Rivers said.

"Now you've wounded me." Hall left the room. The backup man in the Harris tweed jacket stood in the hallway, near the head of the stairs. Hall walked straight at him. The backup man stepped aside. "Not yet?" Hall mumbled at him. The man didn't answer.

Hall stood in the kitchen doorway and watched Denise. She held a glass of white wine in one hand while she gestured with the other. Her back was to Hall and he watched the ripple of muscles in her back. A tall young man with the scars of an old case of acne on his forehead was nodding, almost mesmerized, while Denise lectured on the geopolitical consequences of something or other.

Hall wasn't sure why he hadn't just walked out the front door. There wasn't any face to be saved. He'd been fooled, gulled in a game that was supposed to be played by professionals only.

Perhaps that was what angered him. He couldn't decide whether she was what Rivers said she was, a political staffer who just happened to be in the area doing graduate work, or a new agent with the Company or someone on loan from another agency.

It didn't matter, he told himself. Chances were good that he wouldn't see her after tonight. Unless there was a hunt and she was part of the pack that followed him. And that would not be friendly, what happened then.

Denise must have sensed he was behind her. She looked over her shoulder and smiled and said, "Hello, William." The tall graduate student blinked, the mood broken, and he excused himself and left the kitchen.

"A drink?" There was a jug of white wine in ice in the sink.

"Not tonight," Hall said. "I've got a long drive."

"You don't have to. You can stay here." She took three steps and she was close enough so that he could smell her. A perfume that was partly sandalwood and something else that he thought was anxiety.

"Three in a bed? Me and you and your uncle?" He shook his head. "I feel better in my own territory."

"I'm not his niece."

"I know. It's a term around the Company that Rivers has for the young girls who let him wipe his cock on their chins."

"It's not like that."

"Don't make bets," Hall said. "The night's still young."

"You're talking this way because I made a fool out of you. You're angry with me."

"It's no worse than what I've done to people in my time." He stepped around her and found a glass and drew tap water. He drank it down in one swallow. "That's for the road."

Hall put on his parka and buttoned it. "See you." He went out the back door and down the back steps and circled the house. He was three paces from his BMW when the backup man stepped away from the heavy shadow of an old oak tree. "He said to tell you something."

"Tell me."

"He said to tell you not to dig a hole. He'll find you if it takes ten years."

"And he'd love every month of it?" Hall walked around the man and unlocked the BMW. He started the engine and waited for it to warm up. He extended a hand and touched the litter bag. It had the right weight, the weight of the Python he'd hidden there.

He drove to Blowing Rock with only two stops along the way for coffee. He slept in his own bed that night, wondering just before he went to sleep in which bed Denise slept, and when he awoke early in the morning a heavy fog was rolling up from the Gap, the valley, below.

CHAPTER FIVE

Four days passed. He heard nothing from Rivers or the Company. All Wednesday he watched a late storm brewing. A heavy snow might pin him in the mountains when he needed to move, and move quickly. That afternoon, he readied the house. He packed away clothing he wouldn't take with him and he stored his books in the attic. He plugged the fireplace. Last of all, he emptied the refrigerator and filled two beer boxes with frozen food and perishables.

On the way down the mountain, he dropped off the food and the house key with John Mix. John would care for the house. He'd look in once or twice a week to make sure kids didn't break in and plunder the place. When he arrived at Mix's, there was barely time to deal with the utilities before the offices closed. On Mix's phone, he arranged for the water and the electricity to be switched off. The phone, he told Southern Bell, would be needed until the following Monday. All the bills were to be sent to his lawyer, Joe Bennett, in Winston-Salem.

John Mix followed him from the house and stood on the porch. "You headed any place in particular?"

Hall said he wasn't. "I think I was getting what they used to call cabin fever."

He was halfway to Washington when he ran into the first snow. It was heavy and visibility was limited. When he passed the first snow plow, he left the highway and found a motel and slept for ten hours. He awoke and didn't hear snow plows. He opened the blinds. It wasn't snowing anymore.

He reached Washington before the late afternoon traffic snarl. Or, perhaps because another snow was expected, many people had left work early. A ten-minute drive away from the heart of the city and he reached the Madison Hill Bar and Grill. He passed the bar front and circled the block. He negotiated the cramped driveway that went from the other side of the block into a small lot reserved for the bar employees. There wasn't an open space. Hall parked front bumper to back bumper of a black 1979 Continental with a dented and rusting left rear fender.

He stomped through the kitchen and waved at the startled cooks, as if to say he belonged there and knew all of them. A year before, he might have known them. Jackson's turnover with the kitchen help was a legend. Why work for Jackson and put up with his tirades when you could make the same money somewhere else?

He pushed open the double doors to the bar and stood there until Jackson looked up from his newspaper. The bar was almost empty. Usually, after working hours, during the cocktail hour, the place was a madhouse. Now, with the weather the way it was, it was too early to guess what the day's trade would be like.

"Now I don't have to close," Jackson said. He folded the newspaper and dropped it in a trash barrel behind the bar.

"Pour one, Bilbo," Hall said. Hall had nicknamed him Bilbo after the Senator. When Jackson arrived in Washington in 1976, in the flood of other southerners who crowded the city after the election of Carter, he talked like he had a mouthful of spoonbread. Hall met him then and, though his accent had improved over the years, he'd put the tag on Jackson and refused to peel it away.

Jackson poured a double Jack Daniels that was really a triple and dropped in two ice cubes. "The way you told it, you were going to spend the winter pissing snowballs off your porch into a valley a mile below."

Hall tipped the drink toward Jackson, a salute, and took a long swallow. "I thought you might have heard something."

Jackson leaned forward, his eyes fixed on the bar. "I heard a rumor. It wasn't good. It didn't sound like you, no matter how mad you got."

Hall nodded. "You still see Franklin?"

"He's the one told me. He said some people thought you were talking out of school."

"What did he think?"

"Like I did."

"You know if he's in town?"

"In town," Jackson said, "and at home with a cold, I think."

"Do me a favor. Call him and tell him a visiting redneck is looking for him."

"He'll know?"

"Give him the name Billy Babcock," Hall said.

Jackson hunched over the house phone at the other end of the bar for a couple of minutes. Hall sipped his drink and felt the tension easing in his arms and shoulders. The warmth of the Jack Daniels spread from his toes to the tip of his ears.

Jackson returned. "He said an hour. But not in here. In the parking lot out back."

Hall touched his glass. "One more."

Jackson poured. He poured himself a shot as well and threw it back in one gulp. "What's happening?"

"I'm in a box. It's been nailed together by experts. All but the top. I'm trying to learn to fly."

Hall watched the clock behind the bar. He talked sports with Jackson. The college basketball season about to wind down. The NBA and the baseball season that was only a short time away. During the hour, a dozen or so men and women drifted in. A cocktail waitress checked in and took her place at the serving counter. At the hour mark exactly, Jackson drifted past Hall and pointed at the clock.

"You need a place to stay?"

"I've got to see where I stand first, how bad the pressure is." He dropped a few bills on the bar counter and put on his parka. "See you in a few minutes."

He passed through the kitchen. One of the cooks almost had a heart attack when he heard the door open and close. He was swigging from a wine bottle. Hall grinned and shook his head. Nothing to fear from him. He pushed through the rear door and reached the parking area.

A light powder snow was falling. He stood beside his BMW, hands in his pockets, back hunched. Two minutes later a tan Subaru station wagon plowed down the alley and wheeled and turned broadside to Hall. The window rolled down and Hall could see Franklin's flushed face. He was a big man, thick in the shoulders and the body. Princeton had been his college and he'd played linebacker there.

"Get in," Franklin said.

Hall got into the passenger seat and laughed. Franklin was almost folded up in his effort to fit into the small station wagon.

"Helen's," Franklin explained. "It's goes into four-wheel drive."

"You look like you're wearing it rather than driving it."

There was a huge box of tissues on the dash. Franklin took two tissues and blew his nose. He dropped the wad of tissue into a bag next to his right leg. "You pick a fine time to pull a surprise visit."

"I didn't exactly choose it."

"Anybody knows I've talked to you it's my ass."

"Only Bilbo knows," Hall said.

Franklin looked at Hall with sad, watery eyes. "Heads are starting to roll down the hallways. Yours looks like the first. After that, the list hasn't been filled out completely. I'm watching my back."

"Why you?"

"The mess in Ottawa." A few months back, Franklin led a crew across the border and set up a honeytrap with one of the lower echelon Soviets, one they'd been watching since his posting from the U.N. in New York to the Ottawa Embassy. There had been a feeling about the Soviet early and the pretty boy and the pictures had opened him like a tin of sardines. The product from the entrapment had been good, very good, until it leaked to the Canadians and they hadn't liked the Company working in their backyard space. Questions were asked of the Prime Minister in the Parliament and the story broke in the papers. The Soviet, the object of the honeytrap, was hustled back to Russia and Franklin and his crew barely got over the border ahead of the Mounties. "I've been shuffling papers from one side of my desk to the other since then."

"The whistle. You think it was blown inside the Company?"

Franklin shrugged his shoulders. The movement seemed to set off a loud sneeze. He clawed for a wad of Kleenex. He covered his face. He mumbled, "If it was, it was wasteful."

"And now the Costa Verde operation."

"Some people in the media were making guesses. Your article confirms the extent of the Company involvement there."

"Not my article," Hall said. "It's a ringer."

Franklin lowered the tissues and sniffed a couple of times. "Like I told Bilbo it didn't seem your style."

"I'm thinking of a B and E."

"Where?"

"New York. I want to see the article and I want to see the correspondance with whoever it was pretending to be me."

"I thought you failed breaking and entering at the Farm."

"I'll have help."

"Have Bilbo contact me in a couple of days. I'll be back at the office and I'll see if I can check your file."

"Appreciate it." Hall opened the door on the passenger side of the Subaru. "Watch yourself, pal."

"You can bet the house on that."

In the kitchen, the wine bottle was half empty now. The cook looked like he wanted to giggle. He flipped some strips of bacon on the grill and dropped half of them on the tile floor at his feet.

Jackson saw him enter. He placed a glass on the bar in front of an empty bar stool. He waited with the Jack Daniels bottle in one hand while Hall stripped away his parka.

"Well…"

"Stranger and stranger," Hall said.

The kid must have believed, by God, that he really was a ninja. Dark warrior of death and all that crap.

It was about an hour before first light. Will Hall had had a restless night. It might have been because he was chasing the tail of an idea again, the dangers of too much thinking, or it might have been the mushroom omelet the wino cook had whipped together for him late in the evening.

It wasn't that the kid who was playing ninja was bad at it. Maybe with another year of training, he might have had a fifty-fifty chance of living until lunchtime. As it was, he was good enough to get past the alarm system downstairs and then the locked door at the back of Bilbo's office that led to the rooms upstairs, and then down the creaky hall and then through the locked door to Hall's room without being heard. Hall had accepted the offer of the guest room down the hall from Bilbo's suite above the Madison Hill Bar.

The kid came dressed for the part. All in black and bare-footed and even wearing the hood with only the slit for the eyes. All the trappings.

After grading a hundred on the test so far, the kid stubbed his toe. Literally.

What he banged his toe on was the result of Hall's hurry to get into bed before the booze dissolved all his bones and muscle. He'd opened his suitcase on the floor at the foot of the bed and got out his kit and brushed the Jack Daniels from his teeth. The opened suitcase had remained there, to be ignored until morning and Hall had flopped into bed.

By reflex, the .357 Python was in his hand, eased under one end of the pillow. After five hours of sleep, the alcohol had burned away and he was in his restless. Rolling this way and that.

It was then the kid stubbed his toe. Something rattled in the suitcase. Hall was wide awake in the split instant that followed the sound. His hand knew where the Python was and gripped it, finger inside the trigger guard.

The kid made his second mistake. That was more than a killer usually got. If he'd gone on and tried to do the piece of bloody work he might have made it. Clear-headed, now that the kid hadn't moved, Hall decided the kid was still in training and he believed the Zen crap that was a part of the lessons. He froze with his toe still against the suitcase. Hall guessed the kid was trying to decide whether, in the Zen thinking, the would-be ninja wanted to become a tree or a boulder.

A tree probably, Hall thought, standing straight and blending into a skyline. In his eye, Hall estimated where the kid's chest would be, the broadest part of him. Then he whirled, cocking the Python as he turned and fired three times, as fast as he could pull the trigger. The roar deafened him and the Python had a kick like a jackhammer. Hall rolled off the side of the bed and clawed at the carpet.

He clutched the Python and waited. Enough hearing returned so that he could hear running in the hallway. Bilbo yelled, "What the hell…?"

"Stay there." Silence for some seconds. Then Hall could hear again. He heard a kind of twitching. It didn't sound coordinated. It wasn't crawling or walking and that reassured Hall.

He slipped a hand up the base of the table lamp and switched on the light.

The kid was curled against the wall beside the door. The .357 rounds had messed up his brand-new outfit. He'd been hit once high in the chest and once in the throat. While Hall got to his feet and walked toward the kid. He was dead. Next to him, rammed into the carpet and the floor, was the 24-inch killing sword. Hall stopped beside the sword and touched the blade edge. It was the ninja design, dull on the blade edge. It was for stabbing, not for slicing and cutting.

The door opened. Bilbo stood there in t-shirt and jockey shorts.

"We had a visitor."

Jackson had his look and went downstairs to put on a pot of coffee. Hall showered and shaved and dressed. Then he repacked his suitcase and carried it down into the bar. He placed the suitcase next to the kitchen entrance and placed the Python on the bar next to his right hand.

Bilbo poured strong black coffee into a large mug.

"What was that about?"

"Rivers. You know much about Rivers?"

Bilbo shook his head.

"About four years ago, Rivers got this thing about ninjas in his head. He sent a man to Japan to study with one of the last masters. The man stayed there one year and came back the Company an authority. Maybe like most Americans trying to learn somebody else's game, he only got the outline, the basic lessons. If that boy up there was his star pupil..." Hall let that hang in the air, sounding tougher than he really felt. "The Company decided there were times when silent, stealthy killing was better than handguns and sniper rifles and bombs." Hall had a thought he didn't like. He felt he had to pass it on to Bilbo. "And this stealthy killing, it can look like a lot of things. It can be misdirection. Like tonight. If the kid had got past me, he'd have gone down the hall and got you too. The kid would have taken whatever money there was in the place, anything valuable. The police, after they ran a check on me and found who I was, with some prompting from the Company, would have called it a double murder and robbery. We'd have been another crime statistic in Washington."

A sweat broke on Bilbo's forehead. He turned and grabbed the Metaxa brandy bottle by its long neck and poured a shot in his coffee. He held the bottle toward Hall. Hall shook his head.

"Miles to go before I sleep."

Bilbo sipped his spiked coffee. "What do I do with the guy upstairs?"

"I'll see what the Company wants done with their failures." Hall carried his coffee to the other end of the bar. He turned the phone toward him and dialed the Farm Number.

The duty watch officer answered. "Experimental farm number one."

"This is William Keith Hall. Delta two, delta four, bravo one, fox three."

"Hold a minute." There was half a minute of waiting while the duty officer punched in the name and the identity code and watched the computer for the access. "Yes, Hall. The problem is that your status is vague."

Hall ignored that. "The Madison Hill Bar and Grill." Hall gave him the address and instructions that would get him through the backlot maze and to the rear parking spaces. "I think one of yours ... he was wearing a costume and must have been returning from a dance or something ... well, he fell over a gun and shot himself a couple of times."

"Does he have a name?"

"He's hardly got a head right now. You want to send a housekeeping crew?"

"I'll have to take this higher. You'll be there if housekeeping comes by?"

"What do you mean *if*? The police and the F.B.I. will love this one."

"You'll be there *when* housekeeping gets there?"

That was better. "Sure."

The line went dead. Hall walked down the bar and Jackson got the coffee pot and refilled his cup. Unless the duty officer was being tricky, he'd said that it would take time to get a cleanup crew together. Hall wasn't very sure how much truth a person got from the Farm.

"You going to tell me where you're going?"

"Better you don't know," Hall said.

"You'll be in touch?"

Hall thought about it for a minute. "Not here. I'll call and ask you something. Say, do you cater and how much for spareribs for twelve."

"Spareribs for twelve." Bilbo nodded.

"Then I'll give you an address. You meet me there in fifteen minutes."

Hall finished the coffee. He put on his parka and stuffed the Python in the right pocket. He lifted his suitcase and started through the kitchen; Jackson followed him. At the back door, Hall turned back to face him.

"They might try to lean on you. I don't think they will. Tell them as much truth as you can. The truth always confuses them. They'll think you're lying and they'll spend a lot of energy going off in the wrong directions."

He scraped the windows and got the BMW turned around in the snowfield that the lot was now. The radio, as he drove through the ghost town of early morning Washington, said the highways were clear and the driving conditions good.

CHAPTER SIX

Hall reached New York early in the afternoon.

The winter storm had passed through the city during the night and the cleanup crews were on the streets and the sidewalks as soon as the last snowflake fell. The air was brisk and blustery.

Hall drove around for a time, heading to the east side, until he found a parking garage that suited him. He paid a month in advance and gave a false address and phone number. After the attendant wheeled the BMW away, Hall used the pay phone beside the garage office. This time he called the office number Ben Jacobi had given him.

The woman who answered identified the offices as that of Acme Collections. Hall worked his way past her to the manager.

"What's your business with Mr. Jacobi?"

"Friendly," Hall said.

"Huh?"

"Tell him it's Hall."

Jacobi came on the phone laughing. "You'd be surprised how many people say they're pals of mine."

"What kind of collections do you do there?"

"Easy ones and hard ones."

"Got you." Hall hesitated. "You still need twenty-four hours?"

"That's in the best of all possible worlds," Jacobi said. "Unless it's the popcorn box you said it was."

"You'll want to look it over."

"Not me. A boy of mine."

Hall gave him the address and said that it was the office of *The Truth Seeker.*

"That makes it easy. My pal always wanted to subscribe to that particular paper."

"When will you know?"

"Call me at four."

Hall said he would. He broke the connection and carried his suitcase and his suit bag to the street. He hailed a cab.

The same doorman had worked at the apartment house for the past ten years. He recognized Will Hall as soon as he stepped from the cab. He rushed from the shelter of the lobby hallway and took the suitcase and the suit bag and carried them inside while Hall paid the fare.

"A nasty day," the doorman said.

"Is Mr. Harker using the apartment?"

"No, sir."

They stopped at the doorman's office and Hall fumbled for a five-dollar bill while George Brown, the doorman, got the spare key to the apartment. They made the trade, the key for the five.

"You need help with your bags?"

"Not today."

George nodded. "I'll leave a note for the night man that you're using the apartment."

Hall thanked him and rode the elevator to the fifth floor. It was a corner apartment. On one side it looked down on Riverside Drive. After Hall dropped his bags in the bedroom, he found a bag of fresh coffee beans in the refrigerator and ground a hopper-full while the water boiled. While the water dripped through the filter, he crossed through the living room and opened the door to the balcony. He stood there, feeling the wind and looking down at the river.

Joggers, breathing ragged jets of steam, ran along the walks beside the river. That was tiresome, Hall thought, and he reentered the apartment and closed the door and drew the curtains.

By the time he had showered the coffee was ready. He drank two cups to warm himself. Then he got into the huge double bed and slept exactly two hours.

"According to my man, it's even less than a popcorn box."

"Tonight or tomorrow night?"

"It might as well be tonight," Ben Jacobi said.

"When?"

"Midnight."

Hall gave him the address and said he'd be waiting in the lobby.

"See you then."

Down the street, half a block away from *The Truth Seeker* office, Ben Jacobi dialed the number and let it ring a dozen times or so. He left the phone booth, nodding, and he and Hall walked down the street, away from the blue Buick Fury and the driver. They passed the bar, then the doorway that led to the stairs, and stopped to look in the deli window. It was slow business in the deli. The bar was doing better. The noise of the juke box and the voices carried all the way to the street.

"Me first," Jacobi said. He stepped past Hall and ducked into the doorway that led upstairs.

Hall gave him a thirty second head start. When the count was finished in his mind, he climbed the stairs and stopped at the landing. The whole length of the hallway the offices were dark and deserted. Ben crouched over the lock of the doorway to *The Truth Seeker.* It was so quiet Hall could hear the faint scrape of the lock picks.

Hall put his back to Jacobi. He watched the stairwell. No one followed them. When he turned, he didn't see Ben. The door to *The Truth Seeker* was closed. Puzzled, Hall walked down the hall and stopped in front of the door. The door swung open from the inside and Ben waved him in.

"Easier than we thought." There was a click and Ben directed a beam of light toward the floor. "Where ...?"

"There." Hall led the way into the private office that belonged to Enos Blackman.

It was straightforward writing. What might be called American Standard Prose. It wasn't Hall's prose, his writing, but it wasn't obviously unlike it. It was clean and lean and there was a minimum of window dressing.

The article had been easy to find. It was in a folder on one side of the desk. While Hall read the article, Ben hunched over a file cabinet on one side of the office. It was locked but it was child's play for Jacobi.

The "I" person, the persona that was supposed to be Will Hall, took all the proper credit. In the step-by-step indictment of the Company, the "I" character detailed the tinder-box situation in Costa Verde and sketched the outlines of the three main conflicting elements. The solution, the writer said, was to support the moderate party led by Paul Marcos. It was a position the writer said he had argued with the Company. To prove this, there were quotations from cables and messages that had been sent to the Company.

No, Hall thought. There was no way that he could have remembered the text of those. He'd have needed the messages in front of him. And all those were at the Company. That was the first mistake.

The death of Paul Marcos. A mistake there as well. The writer of the article didn't know that Hall had witnessed the killing from the alley that led to the Avenue San Martin. But the writer knew the sequence. The snipers, the Team, on the rooftop firing the first three shots. Then the smokescreen, the attempt at misdirection, with the use of the gunman on the street level. It was noted that any difference between the ballistics of the rounds fired by the sniper and the gunman would be clouded and lost in the medical service that was controlled by the state, the right wing. True, Hall thought.

The airport. According to the article, Will Hall had been at the air base on other Company business when he recognized the Team. No names were given. Only that it was a killer squad from the Company. There was no mention of the United Mining, Ltd. markings on the plane that took the squad away.

Hall finished the article and replaced it in the file. He was sweating in the chill of the room. He had, he thought, with the help of whoever had written the piece, made himself a lot of dangerous enemies.

"Here," Ben said. He placed a folder in front of Hall. "I think this is what you want."

Hall checked it. A fast flip through and he assured himself that it was the correspondance, originals of letters that he was supposed to have written and carbons of letters from Blackman.

"Lock it up," Hall said. "I'll take these with me."

The driver waited for them down the street. Hall carried the folder under his parka. When they were in the back seat, the driver pulled away from the curb.

"Five bills?" Hall opened the parka and placed the folder on the seat beside him.

"Three," Ben said. "It was too easy. Throw in half a bill for the driver."

Hall took a wad of bills torn his pocket and selected three hundreds and a fifty. At a stoplight, after Jacobi had the money, he reached forward and pressed the fifty into the driver's hand.

"Both of you forget about this one," Hall said.

"Forget what? That I had a couple of drinks with an old friend?" Jacobi patted the driver on the back. "And to make it a good lie, let's have those drinks. Vinnie's."

The driver nodded.

Vinnie's had murals on facing walls. Happy Italian peasants stomped grapes as big as golf balls. There was a strong smell of thick sauces and roasted peppers. Swarthy men sat at the bar and looked straight ahead.

As soon as they entered, Ben gestured at a table for four in an alcove. The owner, bowing over him like he was minor royalty, led the way. Hall followed.

Hall didn't eat. He drank a couple of glasses of the house red wine while Jacobi had a double order of baked stuffed clams and followed that with a huge serving of hay and straw, spinach and white noodles mixed together and covered with a thick sauce of cheeses, cream and butter.

The driver didn't sit with them. He stood at the front end of the bar, a drink in his hand, and watched the front door.

"I wasn't joking," Hall said. "Tonight, this went like rolling out of bed. That easy. But it didn't happen. You know nothing about it. People might get killed."

"Might?"

"Already have," Hall said.

"Who got killed?"

"I think he was Company."

"Ah," Jacobi said," now you've spoiled my appetite."

"At least, now you're listening."

Ben pushed the platter away. Half of the hay and straw had been eaten. "It's fattening anyway," he said.

Ezra Harker, Hall's uncle on his mother's side of the family, had leased the apartment that overlooked Riverside Drive on a yearly basis since the mid 1960's. It had been a hideaway for Ezra during the last stormy affair before old age banked his fires. A bittersweet love, the way Hall heard it. The girl had been a secretary, twenty odd years younger than Ezra. It was only a matter of time before it ended, before the girl found a man her own age and married him. She was, it seems, a girl who did not believe in dead end relationships.

Ezra continued to lease the apartment after the girl was gone. Even now, when he spent most of his time in Winston-Salem, the apartment was cleaned and the shelves and the freezer stocked from time to time.

Years before, when Will Hall was at Yale, Ezra offered him the use of the apartment when he was in New York and it was an offer that continued during his time with the Company. The apartment was his except for any of those in frequent times when business brought Ezra Harker to New York.

The liquor cabinet was well stocked and the wine pantry, temperature controlled, always held a good selection of French and German wines. Recently, his uncle had discovered the Amador County Zinfandels from California.

Hall selected a bottle of the Amador County and found a wedge of Black Diamond cheddar. He sat in the living room, sipped the wine, nibbled at the cheese, and read the thin file of correspondance.

No envelopes. That hardly mattered. It was unlikely the letters had been mailed from anywhere but Blowing Rock. Not after the care with which the box was being put together.

Where the article had been professionally typed the letters to Enos Blackman had been written on an old typewriter. The spacing was uneven, the "f" looked chipped at the base, and the "b" was slightly twisted, bent forward.

He remembered an old Underwood upright that his father kept at the house in Blowing Rock. It was probably still there, stored away in the attic. He didn't remember if there were chipped or twisted letters but he would bet that a good police or F.B.I. laboratory would come up with a match between that old typewriter and the letters.

The letters. Not much there. One, from the contents, accompanied the manuscript. The writer agreed to a lesser cash payment from *The Truth Seeker*. The text revealed that the writer had wanted fifteen hundred dollars and had settled, after some foot dragging, for a thousand dollars.

A second letter complained that the payment had not been received and wondered whether Blackman was trying to welch on the deal.

Another letter, dated a week later, contained an apology. The check had been received and deposited.

The final letter had accompanied a photo that Blackman had requested. The photo that Hall had seen in Blackman's office and recognized as being covertly taken in The Intimate Bookshop in Chapel Hill. Attached to the letter was the barebone biographical sketch. It was accurate enough to have been prepared from the files at the Company.

Born: Sept. 12,1952

High School: Reynolds High, Winston-Salem, N.C. Graduated 1970

College: Yale 1970-74. Degree in history.

Recruited by Company insider. Began training in summer of 1974. Army basic and paratrooper training. Advanced training at the Farm in Virginia completed in 1976. Six months courier duty London.

Posted to Brazil 1976. Posted to Chile 1978. Posted to Costa Verde 1979. Served there until early December of 1980. Recalled after the murder of Paul Marcos. Resignation December of 1980.

He was boxed in tighter than a coffin.

Hall awoke when the house buzzer from the lobby sounded. He was still on the sofa, the letters and the file folder spread in front of him. From the light that came through the balcony window, he could see that it was almost morning.

The night doorman said, "A gentleman down here wants to see you. He says his name is Ben."

Careful, Hall told himself. "Let me speak to him."

"It's important," Jacobi said.

The doorman had the phone again. "Sir?"

"Send him up."

While Hall waited, he cleared away the cheese and the dregs of the bottle of Amador County Zinfandel. Then he pulled aside the curtain at the balcony and looked down at the river. Early joggers ran along the river in the confused light that was half natural and half carbon lamp.

Hall opened the door and let Jacobi in at the first knock.

"You got a drink? Scotch."

While Ben removed his topcoat, Hall found a bottle of Glenlivet and poured a strong one. "Early for you, isn't it?"

Jacobi gulped down half the drink. If he noticed the quality of the scotch, he didn't comment on it.

"What's wrong, Ben?"

"That favor I did for you. It might have been a mistake."

"How's that?"

"Somebody's asking questions."

"Asking questions of you?"

Ben shook his head. "A smalltime mouth I know owes me some favors. He paid off one an hour ago. He told me some very powerful people were asking if a B and E man had been approached in the last day or two by an out-of-towner."

"There's no tie to you?"

"And there won't be." Ben tossed back the rest of the scotch "Everybody knows better than to point a finger at me." Jacobi picked up his topcoat. "You going to be in town for a time?"

"Two or three days," Hall said.

"Give me a call and we'll have lunch at some out of the way place."

Hall shook his head. "Better not, Ben."

"Well," Ben said as he got into his topcoat and buttoned it, "keep in touch."

An hour later, packed again, Hall left the key with the night doorman. He waved down a cruising cab half a block away from the apartment. He decided not to touch the BMW. It was known. Better to leave it stored, out of sight. At the same time, he thought it was safer to avoid planes and trains. Too easy to watch and both were the expected method of transportation.

He directed the cab to the Port Authority and within the hour he caught a bus that took him to Washington.

CHAPTER SEVEN

Hall waited in the motel coffee shop, at a table near the front window. That way he could watch the parking lot outside. A half-eaten chopped sirloin lunch was in front of him. When he saw Bilbo's Continental pull into the parking lot, he dropped his heavy paper napkin on the plate and moved it to the side. Bilbo sat there, frosting the car windows for five minutes before he got out and stood with a gloved hand on the hood of the car. Hall watched the street beyond. As far as he could tell, Bilbo hadn't been followed.

Bilbo entered the coffee shop and sat down at the table. "The spareribs for twelve are in the trunk of the car."

"We pull that another time somebody might get interested. If anybody's listening."

When the waitress passed, Hall ordered a coffee for Bilbo and a refill for himself.

Bilbo moved his gloves aside and made room for the cup and saucer. "Franklin came by the day you left. He wheezed and sneezed all over me."

"What did he want?"

Bilbo sipped his coffee. "What you'd expect. I think the Company sent him around."

Hall smiled. "To give you his cold?"

"To ask some question they wanted asked. Ones that I hadn't answered in any way that pleased them when they dropped by to clean up the mess you made."

One place or the other, that was where Franklin had to be. During the bus trip from New York, Hall had time to think about him. Two or three matters. *One.* After the talk with Hall in the lot behind Bilbo's Bar and Grill, Franklin was in a position to guess that Hall might stay overnight in the guest room upstairs. And that night the boy ninja showed up with his toy sword. *Two.* Franklin knew that Hall was going to try a breaking and entering at *The Truth Seeker* with expert help. Then the questions are asked about a tourist looking for B and E assistance.

On the other hand…

All those were half answers. Not facts. If the Company wanted him, and Franklin told them where he was, they could walk into the Madison Hill and pick him like a ripe cherry. No need for the boy ninja unless they were being fancy. The New York trip rated about fifty percent as well. No reason to go through a time-consuming street rumor search when they could stake out *The Truth Seeker* office and wait for Hall to appear.

More than likely, there hadn't been a betrayal. Or Franklin had made it a partial, half of what he knew so that Hall still had running room. A way of making a few brownie points and, at the same time, hoping that Hall would turn the corners with the proper amount of caution.

If Franklin wasn't informing, then Rivers was running the chase. A chess master, that Rivers. One step behind Hall the whole time and gaining ground. He wasn't the kind to buy the call Hall made to Southern Bell. He didn't take the feint, the misdirection. Any change in the pattern meant that the chase was starting.

"What did you tell Franklin?"

"Nothing. How could I tell him what I didn't know?"

"How about the housecleaning crew?" Hall added a spoon of sugar and stirred the coffee.

"The one in charge had some questions. The same with him. I said you'd left but I didn't know where you'd gone or if you were coming back." Bilbo sipped his coffee and warmed his hands on the side of the cup. "He tried one ploy on me. He did his best to convince me that the boy upstairs wasn't one of theirs. The way he acted, he was doing you and me a favor by cleaning up after you."

"He have a name?"

"If he did," Bilbo said, "he didn't offer it to me."

"Describe him."

"Sandy red hair, six-one, right shoulder lower than the other. I'd say mid-forties."

Hall nodded. "Joe Hargett."

The last Hall had heard about Hargett, he was in Hong Kong "reading" the Chinese refugees. The low shoulder was from a parachute jump in a training mission in Georgia. A sudden gust of wind slapped him against a pine tree and smashed the shoulder.

So now Hargett was back and doing housecleaning. It looked, for a field man like Hargett, to be a demotion. A nudge toward the Exit door.

Hall finished his coffee. Bilbo was waiting. Hall paid both checks and they walked outside. Bilbo put on his gloves and worried the fingers into place.

"I'm chasing my tail," Hall said.

"You trust Franklin?"

Hall hesitated longer than he would have two or three days before. "I used to."

"More or less than you do the others?"

"More, I guess."

Bilbo opened the Continental's door. "Call if you need me."

"Your uncle's sick," Hall said.

"That'll do it." Bilbo laughed. "It's a good change from having to deliver spareribs."

Hall watched Bilbo drive away. When the Continental was out of sight, Hall returned to the coffee shop and got the suitcase and the suit bag from behind the cashier's counter. He stood on the sidewalk out front and waved until a taxi swerved to the curb next to him.

He avoided the big car rental companies. As soon as the Company knew that he'd parked the black BMW and was still moving around, their next move would be a check of the outfits like Hertz. Rent-a-Wreck would be fairly far down on their list.

At Rent-A-Wreck, Hall got a three-year-old Toyota that handled like it had had at least one bad accident hidden away in its past. It was dark green and just anonymous enough on any street so that Hall felt comfortable with it.

He drove across town and found a small motel where he registered as William Keith. He undressed and napped in the dark room until the sky was black and thick outside.

It was a modest row of renovated townhouses. The neighborhood had been changing for years. These were apartments now but it was only a matter of time before the condominium craze touched the owners or the owners sold and the new buyers came in with that in mind. Not that it would matter with Franklin. He owned a place in Martha's Vineyard and another house, a farm that went back to slave times, in Virginia. If the townhouse converted to condominium, if Franklin wanted to remain, it was as simple as moving a bit of money around.

Perhaps that was why Hall wasn't that sorry about the way Franklin had screwed up in Ottawa. A man with his background, his assets, didn't have to struggle to remain with the Company. For Franklin, it was a plaything, a toy, a way of trying out power.

Hall had visited the Franklin townhouse a few times, a few years back. The outside was a modest affectation. Inside, behind the simple exterior, there was enough fine furniture to stock one of the better antique show rooms in London. In fact, a large part of the furnishing had been flown back to the States in a government plane. That was when Franklin and his wife, Helen, had been posted back from London, where Franklin had been attending the Royal College of Defense, the British version of a war college. His cover had been that of a minor official with the State Department. The British tagged him for what he was in half a day.

Hall stood on the landing and looked at the heavy brass door knocker, in the shape of a lion's head. Again, as he had other times, he marveled that someone hadn't ripped it off and sold it as scrap.

Hall lifted the lion's head and knocked twice. He stood straight, directly in front of the door. The light went on and he looked directly at the white glass peephole. There was hardly a hesitation. A lock rattled and the door opened. Franklin stood there.

"Jesus," Franklin said, "I don't know if you should have come here."

"I didn't know about using the phone."

"Who is it?" Helen's voice came from a distance.

"It's alright, dear." Franklin leaned toward Hall. "Where are you staying? I can meet you in an hour."

"The Potomac Motel," Hall said. He added an address.

"Room number?" Franklin looked over his shoulder.

"Meet me in the coffee shop."

"One hour," Franklin said. The door closed and the light went out. Hall returned to the dark green Toyota he'd parked a block away.

Test time.

The Potomac wasn't his motel at all. The Potomac was where he'd met Bilbo earlier in the day.

Test time.

There was an all-night laundromat almost directly across the street from the Potomac Motel. Hall got there fifteen minutes after he left Franklin's townhouse. He parked on a side street and

reached in the backseat for the wad of dirty socks and underwear. He entered the laundromat and dumped the clothing
into a washer. He bought a small box of washing powders from
a vending machine. He fed coins to the washer until it started.
Then he stood at the front, to the side of the plate glass window.
He watched the entrance of the Potomac Motel. Half-an-hour
passed. Nothing happened across the road. He put his laundry in
a dryer and returned to the window.

At the fifty-minute mark it went down. Two black sedans
pulled off the road and into the Potomac's parking lot. One
peeled away and stopped directly in front of the coffee shop. The
other continued and pulled into the curved drive in front of the
motel's lobby entrance. Two men in topcoats got out of the second car and entered the motel lobby at a fast walk.

Hall did the count in his head. He reached fifty when the doors
opened in the back of the first sedan that was parked facing the
coffee shop. Two men scrambled out and slammed the car doors.
In the bright light of the coffee shop entrance, Hall got his look at
those men. One, from his build and the way he moved, was Rivers.
The other, unless Hall was wrong, was the backup man he had seen
with Rivers at Denise's party in Chapel Hill that Saturday night.

After a couple of minutes, Rivers stalked from the coffee
shop and stood on the top step, looking around. Across the
street, Hall wished that he had binoculars. He wanted to see the
expression on Rivers' face. The backup man followed him and
touched Rivers on the shoulder. They crossed the tarmac and got
into the sedan. The driver pulled away from the coffee shop and
parked bumper-to-tailgate behind the other sedan.

Another five minutes passed. The two men who had entered
the motel lobby returned. One stopped at the front sedan and
shook his head. The other walked to the second car and got
into the back seat. After a short time, a brief meeting, the man
returned to the first car and got in. Plumes of exhaust clouded
the two cars as they pulled away from the curb and made a slow

turn and reached the road again. After the two cars went out of sight, Hall left the window and checked the dryer. He dumped the clothing on a table and took his time folding it. When it was done, he carried it to the front window and watched the coffee shop. Another ten minutes passed. There was no sign of Franklin.

A big zero for you, good buddy. You flunked the test.

Not only that. Now Franklin, when he heard from Rivers, would know that it was a test. That would make him dangerous. Soured friends could hate with the best of them. If they'd ever been friends.

Hall returned to his motel and watched TV for an hour or two. Then he slept the restless sleep of a man who couldn't empty his mind. Anger burned the edges of him. The night seemed a week long.

Hall was up early. He had breakfast down the street at a greasy spoon cafe before it was fully light outside. When he left the café, he carried a large takeout cup of coffee. He drove to Franklin's townhouse. He made a pass by first, marking the position of the Subaru station wagon as he went by and looking for any evidence that the Company might have watchers on the street. He saw nothing suspicious. He circled and came back and parked half a block away, across the street from the townhouse. He sipped his coffee. The inside of the Toyota steamed closed around him. The inside of the car was cold and he stamped his feet to keep the circulation going. From time to time, he reached forward and cleared a narrow slit in the condensation on the windshield.

Twenty minutes after Hall arrived at the townhouse, Franklin's wife, Helen, came down the front steps with the little boy.

Around the Company, they joked about the boy and called him the "heir". The couple of times Hall met him, the boy seemed dim-witted and badly spoiled. He was, however, named for Franklin's father and he was an only grandson. The boy, Hall didn't remember his name, was dressed like a little man, in a tailored topcoat and white wool scarf. Under the topcoat, Hall thought, he probably wore the private school's dark blue blazer and charcoal gray trousers.

Helen and the boy got into the Subaru station wagon. After they drove away, Hall watched the street. He finished the last of his coffee and crumpled the cup and dropped it on the floorboards.

He reached under the front seat and drew out the Colt Python. Three rounds in the chambers. One day or other he'd have to stop by his friendly gun shop and pick up some loads. For now, the three rounds would have to do. He jammed the Python in the right-hand pocket of the parka and decided that now was as good as any time.

He banged the lion's head, once, twice. He expected the long wait and the inspection through the peephole. Instead, the door opened immediately and Franklin, in a testy voice, said, "What did you forget this time, Helen?"

That instant Franklin saw Hall and reached for the edge of the door. Hall moved first. He leaned a shoulder against the door and rammed it open. Franklin fell away. Too easily, Hall thought, as he stepped through the doorway and slammed it behind him. Then he saw Franklin heading toward the hall closet. Up there, on the top shelf, that was where he kept the house gun. High on that shelf because Helen insisted that it be kept beyond the boy's reach.

Hall said, "I wouldn't do it," and drew the Python from his pocket. The Python wasn't pointed at Franklin, only in that general direction.

"I'm no fool." Franklin turned slowly and faced Hall.

"Tell me about it."

"What?"

"How you're no fool."

Franklin shrugged. "It's a waste of breath." He waved a hand toward the main part of the apartment. "I've just made a fresh pot of coffee, Maracaibo, this time." Franklin was a coffee nut. It was a game with him. What kind of coffee shall we have this morning? Kenya? Celebes Kalosi? Djimmah?

"I could use another cup." Hall circled him and backed down the hall ahead of him. He reached the kitchen and made Franklin wait while he cleared the table of everything but the sugar dish. Then, still watching Franklin, he got two cups from the cabinet above the kitchen counter and placed them on the table. The coffee grounds had settled in the filter into a hard crust. Hall removed the filter unit and placed it in the sink. He filled two cups and placed one across the table from him. "Have a seat," he said. He lifted the other cup and backed away until he could brace a hip against the kitchen counter. He watched Franklin over the rim of the cup as he drank. The coffee was dark and rich and winy.

"Tell me about it. Waste some breath."

"Last night?" After a swallow of coffee Franklin placed his hands on the table top. "You played a game with me, friend."

"It seemed like a good idea at the time. And even this morning it doesn't look that bad either."

"And if I'd gone there?" Franklin said.

"You'd have found me."

"That true?"

Hall nodded. "I was there."

"Oh, shit." Franklin's face flushed. The cold was almost gone. The flush to his face was shame. "They've got my tail in a crack."

"Write the letter," Hall said. "Look in my file and use my letter as the pattern."

"It's not that easy."

"Give them the fucking resignation. Move to your farm in Virginia and spend the spring counting your money."

"I can't go out that way. Not after the Ottawa mess."

"Why not?"

"Family pride," Franklin said.

That translated: *my father knows about it.* The old man was in a position to follow his son's career. It was the old man's family pride that Franklin was talking about. So much pride that he wouldn't stand for his son to leave the Company with a blot on his copybook. Failure wasn't something the old man understood or tolerated.

Hall nodded. "I guess that explains last night. You wanted to make points with Rivers. "He took another gulp of the Maracaibo. "Rivers is happy with you again and you get to march around in the field and redeem yourself. Then, with your Dad's blessing, you can graduate with honors." Hall finished his coffee and placed the cup in the sink "That explains you. Now, all I want is some explanation of what's happening to me."

Franklin shook his head.

"Make a guess. You've got all that fancy education your Daddy paid for."

"Somebody is gutting the Company."

"Why?"

"If I knew, I'd tell you. Franklin pushed his cup toward the center of the table and nodded down at it. Hall, still careful, filled it and backed away. "Take the mess in Canada. It was handled right. Not a flaw. And the blowup didn't come from the Soviet we'd trapped. It doesn't work that way with them. With us, if we're trapped, we head right for the station chief. It might mean you never work abroad again or that you retire fast. You don't get killed. That Soviet, as soon as he got back to Moscow, got the only hearing he was ever going to have. That was a round in the back of his head. So, he had too much to risk to blow it. And I swear we didn't make a mistake. It was slick as hot goose grease one day and there was sand in the Vaseline the next. And the product..." Franklin pounded a fist into an open hand. "You wouldn't believe how good it was. Right up to the minute we had to run for the border to keep our tails from being kicked."

"Tell me how I fit in this."

"Another way to discredit the Company? All that speculation about the way it was handled in Costa Verde wasn't worth the ink and the paper it was written on. The Company doesn't answer fools, does it? And then an ex-field man named William Keith Hall writes the definitive account of the games the Company played down there, including an account of the Company involvement in the murder of Marcos."

"I've read the article. It's not definitive. The writer missed a couple of points. He didn't know I was there, across the street, when Marcos was killed. And I didn't just happen to be at the military air base when the Team passed through. I was there because Valdez tried to play a word game with me and I got suspicious."

"That's your proof you didn't write the article? Man, you're still in trouble. Those two examples wouldn't help you at all. They're additional evidence and about as damaging as the article itself."

True. Point taken.

"I think I understand last night. My last time through Washington..."

"Rivers had you figured. The disconnect order for the phone didn't fool him. He checked the power company. You see, he has a prediction table on you. When you left Blowing Rock, you'd head for Washington or New York. For Washington, Bilbo is listed as closest friend. I was at the head of the list too. If you reached Washington, you'd contact Bilbo or you'd call me." Franklin grinned. "You know what?"

"What?"

"He says the ninja wasn't his."

"That's hard to believe."

"It burned his ass you thought the ninja was his. He said if it had been one of his, you'd never have got past him. And he was put out that you had the Company do the housecleaning."

Hall laughed.

"He was English. At least he was on an English passport. He'd flown into New York five days earlier. The day you arrived in Washington; he flew in on the shuttle."

"How'd Rivers get all this?"

"A check of all the cars around the Madison Hill Bar. He had to get there somehow and he had to plan on a way to leave. A walkaround crew found a car on the side street near the entrance to the alley that leads to the parking behind the Madison Hill. What caught their attention was a trench coat and a pair of foul weather boots on the front seat. And it was a rental car."

Hall nodded.

"He got a name and an address from the car rental agency. A motel. There he found luggage and the Brit passport."

"The ninja have a name?"

"Can we go into the living room?"

"Alright." Hall watched Franklin get to his feet. Not a false move. Hall kept his distance. They reached the living room. Franklin stopped in the center and pointed at the telephone table.

"The back page of the phone book."

Hall flipped the heavy phone book and opened the back cover. It was there, written in light pencil. So that it could be erased later, Hall thought.

There was a pad on the phone table. Hall tore off a sheet and used the pen from the holder. Winford Boyle. That and an address on Tedworth Square. "What's Tedworth Square?"

"I checked it. It's in Chelsea. A couple of blocks off King's Road."

"This is straight?"

"Cross my heart and hope to resign." Franklin shook his head slowly side to side. "Until the pressure got to me, I was trying to help you. This is as far as I got."

"Call it even," Hall said. "This against last night."

"It's the nature of the business."

Hall folded the sheet of note paper and placed it in the left pocket of his parka. He shoved the Python in his right pocket. "This time you haven't seen me."

"After last night? The way I see it, after what I did last night, you wouldn't come within a mile of me."

Hall backed toward the hall. Franklin followed but kept his distance. Hall stopped one step from the front door. "Unless I wanted revenge."

Franklin shook his head. "Like they say, that's a dish better eaten cold. That's what Rivers would expect of you."

There was a scrape of a key. It was so sudden that Hall didn't have a chance to step away. The door slammed into his back and threw him off balance. It was Franklin's chance if he wanted it. Instead, hands to his sides, he backed away and shook his head.

Helen stepped through the doorway. "Sorry, I didn't ... Will, is it you?"

"In the warm flesh." He bowed slightly toward Helen. "Good to see you. I just dropped by to have a coffee with Franklin."

"Can you stay? I can fix us a breakfast ..."

"Can't this time." He waved and stepped around Helen and pulled the door closed behind him. He heard Helen raise her voice in a question and he heard Franklin's hard tone smashing at her. Then there was silence.

After Hall checked out of the motel, he drove the rental car to New York and arrived in the middle of the afternoon. There was time to conduct some financial business with a Dime Bank where he kept an account he didn't think the Company knew about. He turned in the rental car and took a cab to the British Airways office, where he booked a flight to London. At a pay phone down the street, he called Harker Industries. A few minutes of conversation with his uncle's executive assistant and he was assured that a call would be made within the hour and that Ezra's London apartment would be available to him when he arrived there the next morning.

CHAPTER EIGHT

It was late afternoon. Hall's body felt like it was midnight. It was his first day in London and he'd stayed at the Harker-owned apartment only long enough to shower and change clothes.

He was on Craven Street. The building was old. There was a brass marker outside. Heinrich Heine had lived there when he was in England. The building was also the home of the Craven Club. Hall stepped into the dark hallway and climbed the stairs. The key to the second-floor door was in his pocket. He'd found the key where he'd left it, in the locked drawer in the Harker flat where he kept a few books of traveler's checks and some stacks of English money.

The key fitted, he turned it in the lock and pushed the door open, and he stepped inside the Craven Club. It was a private club, a way around all the odd opening and closing hours the public lounges had to follow. A private club could serve all day and half the night.

It was early. Not much of a crowd. One couple at the bar and a blonde woman twenty years younger than the gentleman she was with nuzzled his neck at one of the low tables and chairs spaced about the room.

Hall stood at the end of the bar until the bartender came to him. Hall gave his name. "I've been out of the country," he said. "I thought I'd see if my dues are paid up."

⚜   ⚜   ⚜

He was on his second gin and tonic when the Air Vice Marshal entered. He was retired now and had been for the better part of two years. With the cutback of the Royal Air Force he'd seen the handwriting on the wall. Five years to go before retirement and with all the talent and ability in the world he'd known he'd never be promoted to Air Marshal. So, he'd put in his retirement and gone into business.

A tall man in a well-cut suit. Gray hair and green eyes. The long bony face of a Scotsman.

"Mac, how are you?" Hall stood and held out his hand.

"Willie." Mac liked to call him Willie just to see if it would fluster him. Mac slumped into the chair next to Hall and eyed the barmaid who was walking toward their table. "Done this one yet, Willie?"

Hall laughed. "Give me time. I just got to town."

Mac ordered a double of the single malt scotch and watched the barmaid's hips. "Might not be worth the trouble," he said.

Over the first drink, the talk was about Mac and how his life was going. Business was good. He'd taken a good position with an electronics firm that did a lot of work with the government. Tracy was fine too, the best marriage a man could make. When they talked about Tracy, there was a hard glint in Mac's eyes. Hall had introduced them in Washington and, half-joking, Mac used to complain that Hall had palmed off one of his old girls on him. That was before Mac loved her. After they were a pair, it didn't matter. Still, when the mood was on him Mac liked to fall back into the posture of an injured man.

It was Mac who'd introduced Hall to the Craven Club one afternoon and he'd vouched for Hall when he decided to join. The story Mac told, perhaps fanciful, was that the Club had been founded by some intelligence types from over on Northumberland, not far from Craven Street. They'd wanted a place where they could unwind over a few drinks without feeling they were under the public eye. Over the years, in time, the membership broadened. "Back then," Mac said," we called this Spook Haven."

In return, Mac had been introduced to the Madison Hill Bar and Bilbo by Hall. That was during the time after Mac fell in love with Tracy and he was flying the Royal mail plane from London once a week. He volunteered for the flight so he could push his courtship with Tracy.

Over the next drink, Hall told Mac what was happening to him. Mac didn't seem surprised. He murmured that he had heard part of it from one of his old contacts. He said he'd pooh-poohed it with the contact. Not like my American friend at all, he'd said.

"You have that contact still or did you duel over my honor?"

Mac grinned. "I might have convinced him."

Hall took the slip of paper from his pocket. On it was written the name of the ninja boy and the address on Tedworth Square.

Mac took the paper and stared at it. "Winford Boyle? A Winford Boyle doesn't sound like he belongs on Tedworth."

"A young fellow," Hall said. "He tried to ninja me in the guest room over the Madison Hill."

"Tried? Where's he now?"

"If nobody claimed him, he's in Potter's Field by now."

"You don't look bruised."

"He didn't get close enough."

Mac folded the paper and placed it in his jacket pocket. "You American types have all the fun these days."

"It wasn't all the fun you think it was."

"Spoken just the way John Wayne would have."

"Another?" Hall nodded at the barmaid.

"This drink needs company," Mac said.

Hall waved at the barmaid. She brought the drinks and smiled at Mac. Mac watched her walk away. "This is the last one," he said. "She's beginning to look good to me."

The Harker flat in London was on Walton Place, directly behind Harrods. While Hall waited to hear from Mac, he walked around Knightsbridge like a tourist. He had dinner at a place on Beauchamp Place and later stopped in at the Grove pub down the street for a pint. It was cold and drafty in the Grove and too crowded near the fireplace. Hall stood near one of the portable heaters and drank his bitter and listened to the voices and thought, it is a long trip for a pint if this whole matter becomes a dead end.

He had a good night of sleep, though his body clock was still confused. He was sitting over coffee and buttered toast when the flat buzzer sounded.

It was Mac. "You got some coffee for a man who's been out freezing his buns on your business?"

Hall poured coffee in the living room and added more toast and jam for Mac. Mac shucked his topcoat and sat down at the coffee table. "Tracy doesn't believe you're in town. She thinks I've taken up with a tart while she's in the country."

"Give me her number and I'll call," Hall said.

Mac scribbled the phone number and passed it across the table. "But it's not really necessary. It keeps a woman off balance to think another woman might want what she's got to herself."

Hall placed the number beside the phone. "Find anything, Mac?"

Mac wedged a piece of toast in his mouth and dug a small leather notebook from his jacket pocket. "It seems our boys have been looking for this one ourselves. He was on his way to being a bad one and we wanted to stop him before he got there." Mac placed the notebook on the table and licked butter and jam from his fingers. "It could be you got this information because my contact considers you've done us a favor." Mac opened the pad. "His real name was Winford Baines. Born in Belfast and learned some of his rough trade on the streets there. He dropped out of sight four years ago. He'd been implicated in the fire-bombing of a

British Army truck. Two dead. He was still on a list they keep over there. There was some indication that he'd decided that, while he believed in freedom and all that, he felt he could make a good living at what he'd been learning as a hobby." Mac chewed another wedge of toast while Hall refilled his coffee cup. "There was a rumor, about the time the Shah fell, that Baines was involved in the killing of one of the Shah's cousins over on Belgave Square. Remember that one? Something out of a James Cagney roaring twenties film? Shotguns blazing away from a car when the Shah's cousin and his bodyguards came out of his flat. That one and maybe two or three other jobs. A jealous older type who didn't like the fact his young wife was seeing a French playboy. Exit the playboy. A disenchanted Hungarian diplomat who was edging toward your boys. Done with a blade in a crowded underground near the Sloane Square station. By the time people discovered the Hungarian wasn't having a heart attack or a stroke the killer was long gone."

"Three jobs in four years? It doesn't sound like steady work."

Mac grinned. "Those are the ones they're fairly certain they can tie him to. He's no Carlos but he takes his work seriously. They may be a few other jobs we haven't heard about."

"That the whole package?" Hall watched Mac close the notebook.

Mac shook his head. "The address on Tedworth. What did you notice about Boyle or Baines?"

"Young. Like a boy."

"That's it. The address on Tedworth. The flat is owned by an old poof named Lester. Raymond Lester. You know what a poof is?"

"Homosexual," Hall said.

"Our boys were over in the area last night asking questions of the neighbors. It seems that Raymond Lester had a young nephew living with him the last three or so years."

"What does Lester do?"

"Newspaperman. Says he's a writer. Must have inherited some money years back." Mac pulled back the cuff on his right arm. He checked his watch. "I made an assumption you might have some false identification with you. Something that ties you to the American Embassy."

"I do." There was an I.D. card that he'd used once on a courier trip from Washington to London. It was, he thought, still in the locked drawer with the traveler's checks and the cash. He went into the bedroom, unlocked the drawer and returned with the identification folder.

"A man with I Branch has an appointment with Lester for half-ten. I arranged it so you could come along. Might be you'd only want to listen. On the other hand, you might slip in a question if one comes to you."

At ten exactly, the door buzzer sounded. The man from I Branch was waiting outside with his car and driver.

John Tobin was short and barrel-chested. He wore a dark suit, a tweed hat and a trench coat. A bulldog pipe was clenched so tightly in his teeth that it seemed a part of his costume.

The driver took them by a roundabout way from Knightsbridge to King's Road. Mac sat on one side of Tobin and Hall on the other. A slow, dull rain, as slick as oil, coated the windshield.

Tobin spoke with the pipe in the center of his mouth. "I understand, Mr. Hall, that we have you to thank for the bit of business in Washington."

"The boy got fancy for some reason," Hall said.

Tobin looked at Mac. Mac nodded his head toward Hall.

"I think he was expanding his repertoire. He was trying with a short killing sword."

"Lucky for you." Tobin sucked at his dry pipe. "He was better than most with a handgun."

They reached King's load. A mile or so down the Road and the driver turned onto Smith Street. Directly ahead, in the distance was the Royal Hospital, the home for retired military men. One block down Smith the driver took a right and then a left and they were on Tedworth Square. A small fenced-in garden was in the center of the square. The car passed the garden and took another right. To the left, on one of the round blue markers on a building front, was MARK TWAIN, AMERICAN HUMORIST, LIVED HERE 1896-97.

The driver pulled to the curb and braked.

"This one," Tobin said. "We're early."

It was a row of newly renovated flats. A bow window was on the flat at the first level. White curtains covered the inside of the window. As Hall stepped from the car, he saw a face and a movement beyond the glass and the gauze. Then the curtain fluttered and the face was gone.

Raymond Lester reminded Hall of Rivers. An older, feeble and effeminate Rivers. The thin, sickly chest and the matchstick arms. The difference was that there wasn't a mean bone in Lester. In fact, all the fires seemed to have died in him. He looked to be about a hundred and fifty pounds of cold ashes.

John Tobin began the questioning. He'd introduced Mac as his associate and Hall was, he said, a representative of the American government. According to him, Hall was there because Lester's nephew had died a violent death in Washington and the United States wanted to know exactly what Winford Boyle was doing in that country.

At the proper moment, Hall took the I.D. folder from his pocket and held it toward Lester. From the way Lester's eyes glazed over and flickered the Embassy identification might as well have been a gas credit card.

"He was on holiday," Lester said.

"This time of the year?" Tobin asked.

"He said ... said ... there was a special fare."

"He was not there on business?" Tobin turned to the side and warmed his hands in the glow of coals in the fireplace.

"He was unemployed."

"Odd." Tobin turned. He rubbed a warmed hand across his brow. "His account at Barclay's shows a rather healthy balance."

"He had ... independent means."

Tobin lifted an eyebrow at Lester. The question was there.

"From an aunt's estate, I believe," Lester said.

"Would you have her name and the name of the solicitor who handled the estate?" Tobin took an envelope from the inside pocket of his jacket and poised a pen over it.

"I ... don't remember."

"You know, I assume, that your nephew died while attempting to commit a violent crime?"

It was as if iced water had been poured over Raymond Lester's head. The shock tore at him. From his position at the side of Lester, Hall realized that this moment had been planned. Lester had only been told that Boyle had died a violent death. He had not, it seems, been told any of the circumstances of the death.

"A violent crime?" Lester's hands came together and fumbled, as if he couldn't quite get the fingers laced together.

"He attempted to kill a minor American government official," Tobin said.

"I don't believe ..." It was the last gasp, the final defiance.

Mac rubbed a hand over his face and looked down at the coals in the grate.

"Mr. Boyle was not exactly kin, was he?" Tobin said.

"He was ... a close friend. A young man who needed help."

"And there was no income from an aunt's estate?"

Lester shook his head.

"Do you know where he received his income?"

"He refused to tell me. I asked him a number of times."

"Did that make you suspicious?"

"I was apprehensive," Lester said.

"If we make the assumption that Mr. Boyle was, to some extent, involved in some kind of shady business, how was contact made with him? By mail, in person, by telephone?"

"He received mail here at the flat and he had his own telephone in his room."

"Did he have visitors?"

Lester shook his head. "Not that I'd know about. But, then, three afternoons-a-week I'm on the Strand with the magazine I edit."

"Which magazine is that?"

"Actually, it's a journal," Lester said. "*Nature's Way*. It concerns itself with health food."

"Did Boyle travel often?"

"Once-a-month. Or every two months. He was away a week or ten days each time."

Tobin shifted his feet slightly, until he was facing Hall. "The gentleman from the States may have a question or two to ask of you."

"Did Mr. Boyle have any close friends that he saw often?"

Raymond Lester shook his head.

"A pub where he was a regular?"

"Not that I know about." Lester reached in his jacket pocket and brought out a package of Weights. He lit one. "We had a drink now and then at The Queen's Head."

"Did Mr. Boyle talk about his work?"

"He was close about his business. If he had any business at all. I have trouble believing that he did."

"How did you meet Mr. Boyle?"

"If I can remember correctly it was at the pub I mentioned earlier. The Queen's Head."

At the end of the interview, Tobin asked if they could look at Winford Boyle's room and his things. Lester said that he was willing to allow Tobin to look about but he wasn't going to make a circus of the matter. The other two, he said indicating Mac and Hall, would have to wait in the living room or the car outside.

Mac said, "I could use a breath of air," and he and Hall said their good days to Raymond Lester and moved outside to wait.

"I know the pub," Mac said. They stood on the walk and smoked. "In my continuing quest to have at least one pint in every pub in London, I wandered in there by mistake one night. It's a poof bar."

"A place where Boyle might make his contacts?"

"I doubt it," Mac said.

It was ten minutes before Tobin came from the flat. He motioned Mac and Hall into the car. The driver pulled away from the curb and headed for Flood Street. Tobin said, "One matter might interest you, Mr. Hall."

Hall leaned forward.

"I found a wad of receipts on the bureau, from a trip Boyle or Baines or whatever his name was took recently to Ireland. Round trip by train to and from Fishguard. The ferry to Ireland. A rental car waiting for him there. A receipt for a room where he stayed one night. At the Keep in Kinsale."

"The Keep?"

"I think it's a restored castle there," Mac said.

"Or part of a castle," Tobin said. "I've seen it in the tourist books."

"You think it might have been a meeting of some kind? Where he made contact?"

Tobin smiled. "Or another boyfriend," he said.

CHAPTER NINE

Mac, when he realized Hall actually was considering following the cold fox trail to Kinsale, offered to drive him to Fishguard. There Hall could take the ferry to Ireland. It was a tempting offer, a chance to spend a few more hours with a good friend, but Hall resisted until he returned to his flat and put in a call to Kent.

Tracy answered at once. "Willie, is that really you?"

"In the jetlag flesh."

"Is Mac with you?"

"Mac?" Hall turned and looked at Mac who was seated on the sofa, his long legs crossed, and a wide grin on his face. "I haven't seen a thing of him. Is it true he's got himself a London tart? A Swedish girl over on Park Lane?"

Mac chuckled.

"Honestly..." Tracy sputtered. "When are you two going to grow up?"

"I hear she's a beauty. All of seventeen and with long blonde hair."

"Where did you hear about her?" Tracy sounded serious all of a sudden.

"The old boy network. It's the talk of London."

"Let me speak to Mac, Willie."

"When and if I see Mac..."

"Willie..."

Hall turned and held the receiver toward Mac. "Well, what do you know? Mac just walked in. He looks tired and a bit tipsy."

Mac took the receiver and said, "Hello, sweetheart."

Hall entered the kitchen and got two cans of Swan from the refrigerator. He remained there for a time, sipping his beer for the can, giving them time to get the best or the worst of it over. He found two glasses and carried them and the cans of beer into the living room. Mac was cooing into the phone. "Here's the troublemaker." Mac passed the receiver to Hall and took the full can of beer and the glass and sat on the sofa.

"When are we going to see you, Willie?"

"I've got to make the crossing to Ireland. Either tonight or in the morning."

"Tell her I'm considering making the journey with you," Mac said.

"You're not," Hall said.

"I need a vacation. I'm working too bloody hard at this retirement job."

"You tell her."

Hall uncoiled a length of extension cord and passed the phone to Mac. Mac took a huge swallow of Swan and said, "Look, love, Willie's in a bit of a scramble. I think it might be dangerous, him there alone the way he is." He listened for half a minute or so, nodding. "That's hardly true. The two of us can take on the whole Russian army and you know it. And here's another convincing argument. If anything happens to Willie, who's going to be godfather to our firstborn?"

"Firstborn?" Hall opened his eyes wide.

Mac winked.

"Is that why Tracy's in the country?"

Mac nodded. "Two days at the most," he said into the phone. "And I'll bring you back a lovely present. Waterford glass? A bit of lace?" A hesitation and then Mac laughed. "Of course, I'm trying to bribe you."

Hall sipped the Swan.

"And I'm certainly not interested in any Irish girls. Have you seen what passes for an Irish girl in Ireland? All the real beauties moved to London." He listened, nodding. "I'll call you when we arrive and let you know we're fine. Take care of the two of you."

Mac placed the receiver on the hook and let out a long hiss of breath.

"Your firstborn?"

"I meant to tell you but it must have slipped my mind."

"At your age, Mac?"

"The blood line tells," Mac said.

The train arrived at Fishguard near sundown and was shunted onto a track near the ferry pier. Both Mac and Hall had packed for light travel. They lined up and passed through the customs shed within twenty minutes of leaving the train. Below them, as they stood on the main deck, dozens of cars were driven into the belly of the ferry.

Mac found the bar on his first try. "By the good smell of it," he explained. Hall stood aside and watched Mac wedge himself into a space at the crowded bar. He brought back doubles of Irish. They were sipping those, warming themselves after the passage through the customs shed, when they felt the shudder and the ferry moved away from the pier.

"You have your sea legs, Willie?"

Hall lifted his eyes from his drink and looked across the room. A thick-chested man with graying hair, wearing a belted tan trench coat, his back to the bar, was staring at Hall. Their eyes caught and the man turned away.

"Something...?" Mac looked across toward the bar.

Hall shook his head. "I don't know about my sea legs."

"Rough seas out here now and then." Mac waited while Hall finished his drink. Glasses held in one hand, elbows out like a football player, he dipped into the crowd and headed for the bar again.

❧   ❧   ❧

By ten that night, the passengers had settled in for the long voyage. The lights were dimmed in the second-class seating compartments and most of the people were trying to sleep. Hall was restless. He'd tried sleep and that had been impossible. His knees were stiffening. He stood and stretched his legs. Mac, from his seat to his left, stirred and blinked at him.

"Going on deck," Hall said. "The air's used up down here."

"Right with you … or behind you," Mac said.

Hall struggled into his parka as he moved down the aisle between the even rows of sleeping people. He reached the lobby and the wide staircase that led to the deck. The ferry lurched under him and he caught the railing and used it as he climbed the staircase.

A raw wind blew across the deck. Hall walked a distance from the doorway and huddled in the shelter of a lifeboat and used the shield of it to light a cigarette. The gusting wind almost blew the cigarette from his hand. He took two puffs and then walked to the rail. He tossed the butt over the side. Lights from the cabins and compartments below lit the sea. There was a white boil and churn along the side of the ferry.

Hall heard the door to the deck open. He turned. "That you, Mac?"

He saw a blur of pale cloth. A tan trench coat. Not Mac. Mac was wearing a dark blue lined raincoat that was almost military issue.

"Mac?" The man stopped a couple of feet from Hall. "Afraid not." Closer, Hall could see gray streaks in the man's hair. "Stifling below, isn't it?"

"Yes."

"Perhaps a bit of chill will wake me." The man opened his trench coat and removed it. He tossed it up, onto the lifeboat cover. Under the coat he wore a heavy black turtleneck sweater. "You have a light? I'm afraid I've used the last of my matches."

"Too much wind," Hall said. "Here." Hall dug the lighter from his parka pocket. "Light your own."

The man stepped forward and extended a hand. At that moment, Hall remembered him. The man in the trench coat who'd been watching him from the other side of the bar.

"Damn." The man seemed to lose his balance, as if the ferry had moved under his feet. The hand that reached for Hall's lighter grazed his hand. It grabbed at hall's parka sleeve.

"Hey, watch it." Hall spread his legs to distribute his weight evenly. The man slammed against him.

"Sorry, I can't seem to get my ..."

Hall could smell whisky on the man's breath and the scent of some kind of garlic sausage. He realized the man's weight and strength were forcing him toward the ship's railing. The man's other hand, his left, pinned Hall's arm to his side. Hall tried to lean forward and force a shoulder in the man's chest. The man turned slightly to avoid it. Hall slammed hard against the rail and felt it in his kidneys.

A door opened in the distance. There was a flash of light and then darkness again. The man looked over his shoulder. His breath was ragged. A grunt as the man mustered his strength. Hall's left foot was lifted from the deck. Hall reached back and grabbed the rail with his left hand. The rail was wet with spray and freezing and Hall didn't know how long he could hold on.

There was a blur in the corner of Hall's eye. A tall man faced him beyond the man in the black turtleneck. An image of pale skin. Then Mac stepped forward and grabbed the man by the back of his sweater and the seat of his pants and threw him overboard. Hall almost went with him. He was pulled that way by the final desperate grab. Mac caught Hall by the shoulders and wrapped him in a bear hug.

"Willie, what have you been up to? Kissing strange men on the deck of a ferry in the Irish Sea? What will you do next?"

THE SPY IN A BOX

"It was more like dancing," Hall said. He struggled for his breath.

Mac backed away from the rail, taking Hall with him. "Who was he?"

"I don't know. Somebody I saw watching us from across the bar."

"You didn't mention it."

"It didn't seem important at the time."

"Ready to go below?" Mac released Hall and watched to see if he was steady.

"Yes." A step and Hall remembered. "A second." Hall walked to the lifeboat and felt along the cover until he found the tan trench coat. "He left this."

"You're getting a chill." Mac took the coat from Hall and followed him to the doorway and down the staircase to the cabins.

❧ ❧ ❧

"Here." Mac dug around in the side pocket of his carry bag and found a silver flask. "Have a taste of this."

They were back at their seats. No one around them stirred. In the dim light, the airless room, there was snoring and blubbering and wheezing.

Hall uncapped the flask and had a swallow of pure fire. It had the mild smoke of a single malt scotch in it. Hall lowered the flask and offered it to Mac.

Mac said, "Have another."

Another swallow and Hall could feel the heat in the pit of his stomach. The shivering had almost passed. He thought he'd recovered from the cold or the danger.

Mac took the flask and wedged it between his thigh and the side of the seat. The trench coat was spread over his knees. "American made." He pointed at the manufacturer's patch.

89

"Harbor Master." He lifted the flask and sipped the scotch. He passed the flask to Hall. Hall capped it and held it.

Hall watched Mac turn the coat and empty the side pockets. "Kents. One open packet. One full." He placed the cigarettes on the seat beside him. "One box of Swan matches." A twisted wad of papers followed. Mac smoothed the papers and struck a match. "Car rental from London to Fishguard." He put that paper aside. "Ferry ticket. First class." Mac stuffed the cigarettes and the papers in the coat pockets. He patted his way across the rest of the coat. He stopped at a place high on the inside right of the trench coat. "What do we have here?"

It was a zippered pocket. Mac pulled the zipper downward. He reached inside the pocket. "Bingo. Isn't that what you Americans say?"

First a passport. Then a tan envelope without writing on the outside of it. Hall took the passport and held it open while Mac struck a match "American. Warren Blair Baker. Hometown is Copper City, Utah."

Mac dropped the match before it burned his fingers. He stepped on it and lit another one. Hall flipped through the pages. Entry after entry. "He's been a busy little bugger," Mac said.

Hall closed the passport and put it in his pocket.

Mac passed Hall the Swan matches. "You light one." Mac opened the tan envelope. "Traveler's checks and cash." Mac flipped quickly through the traveler's checks. "Roughly five hundred pounds. There was a flat sheaf of new money. Twenty- and ten-pound notes. "About three hundred pounds," Mac said.

"What do we do with this?"

"Dump the checks and spend the pounds. In fact, first chance we get we'll have a drink to the bugger."

A few minutes after one a.m. the ferry docked at Rosslare. Before they left their seats, Mac wadded the trench-coat into a ball and stuffed it under a seat on the other side of him. They left the huge seating compartment and joined the line in the inner deck outside the cabin and waited until the gangway was in place and the doorway opened.

CHAPTER TEN

Two hours, and a bit after they left Rosslare in the rental Escort, they passed through the dark and sleepy village of Kinsale. From the instructions given over the phone, Mac took the right fork at the end of the main street and they climbed a high and winding road that took them to the entranceway of The Keep.

A light burned in the parking area outside. A Cortina, two other Escorts and a black Mercedes sedan lined the gravel space that fronted the high stone arch that led to The Keep.

As instructed, Mac pulled the rope on the right side of the door. A bell rang in the distance.

They were registered by an effeminate blond young man with only the pale whisp of a beard. "You spoke to my father when you called. He wasn't feeling well so I waited up for you." The light was on in the dining room beyond the lobby. A sleek-haired Irish boy in his teens sat at a table there drinking white wine. He had bad skin and two teeth were missing in the upper front of his mouth.

"There are only twelve rooms in The Keep," the young man told them as he led them up the stairs "It's out of season. Usually you wouldn't find a vacancy."

They were registered in rooms 11 and 12 on the fourth level of the hotel. The walls of the staircases and the halls were papered with hunting scenes and the floor, creaking gently under their feet, was carpeted with heavy pile. There were four rooms on each level and a bathroom with each.

THE SPY IN A BOX

When they were left to themselves, after the footfall of the young man faded into the levels below, Mac stuck his head into Hall's room. "Almost half three now. Let's give them two hours."

Hall stretched out on his bed and closed his eyes. He was fully clothed except for his shoes. It seemed he'd hardly closed his eyes when he felt a hand on his shoulder.

Mac leaned over him. "Time," he said.

The registry book was still on the counter beside the door that led outside. While Mac watched, Hall flipped through the book. He reached the present. A Mr. and Mrs. Carl Hubbard from Washington, D.C., U.S.A. were registered in rooms 1 and 2. Two rooms for a married couple? Even out of season it seemed an extraordinary expense. Another couple, the Tindles from Gravesend.

Something strange about the name the American couple had. Carl Hubbard? Wasn't that the old screwball pitcher for the Dodgers? Maybe not, but it was something close. Close enough to make a person wonder if it wasn't based on it.

Hall closed the book and joined Mac. He was about to tell Mac what he's learned when an overhead light in the lobby flared on. "Is there something I can do for you, gentlemen?" A tall man in a bathrobe stood in a doorway to the side of the lobby, near the dining room. He wore his hair close-cropped and his thick mustache was reddish gray.

"We wondered..." Mac began.

"We hoped your son might still be awake," Hall said. "After the ferry ride and the car trip we're too tired to sleep."

"And you wanted...?"

"A dram or two of your best," Mac said.

"It's past hours," the man said. "But you are guest and I could say it was for your health." He led them across the lobby to the bar. He unlocked the door and switched on a lamp. He placed three glasses on the bar. "Jameson black?"

"Beautiful," Mac said.

"I'm your host, Thomas Hinson." Hinson poured. "No ice, I hope."

"I'd as soon drown my mother," Mac said.

"One never knows about Americans," Hinson said.

"I trained this one myself." Mac laughed.

Hall lifted his glass and drank. "Your health, gentlemen."

There was little talk over the drinks. Mac allowed himself to be nudged into telling Hinson some lies about why he was in Ireland. "A nephew at medical college in Galway," he said. "And a chance to show my American friend around."

"The colleges in Scotland aren't good enough?" Hinson said.

"Oh, no." Mac seemed surprised that Hinson had read his accent so easily. During his time in the R.A.F. he'd acquired a better than average covering English accent. "The boy...poor lad...he's not bright enough." Mac tapped the side of his head.

A second drink finished; Hall was ready to pay.

"They'll be added to your total," Hinson said. He followed them from the bar and switched off the light and locked the door. Then, for the first time, he seemed to notice that neither Mac nor Hall were wearing shoes.

Mac lifted a stockinged foot and grinned, "We didn't want to wake your other guests," he said.

"Our thanks again." Hall started up the stairs. Mac was right behind him. Halfway up the first flight, Hall turned and looked down at Hinson. Hinson glanced from them to the guest book on the counter. He was headed in that direction when Hall climbed three more steps and went out of sight.

At the landing between the second and third levels, Hall stopped and touched Mac on the arm. Mac leaned toward him.

"I've got a hunch," Hall said. "Hinson knows now why we were down there and he's doing the same thing."

Mac lifted an eyebrow.

"He's checking the book to see who we are and where we're from."

"And...?"

"We'll wait and see."

After a minute or so, they could feel movement on the stairs, Hinson's footpace. Hinson reached the top of the first flight and paused. He was in the hallway that led to rooms 1 through 4. Then he was moving again, the slippee-slip of his slippers. When that sound ended, there was a knock on a door. Two raps, a wait and two more.

A door opened. The voice had a northeast twang and the faint whine of an American. "Yes, Hinson? This had better be important."

"You asked me to tell you..." The door was closing. "Two men registered early this morning. A Mr. Duncan MacIntosh, a Scot, and the other is American..." The door closed and Hinson's voice was cut off.

Hall let the voice of the American man echo in his mind for a time. It found a face. Rivers. The voice fitted Rivers. That was interesting.

Hall nodded at Mac. They finished the climb to the fourth level. Mac stopped at room 11. "I think there's a drop or two left in the flask."

Hall shook his head. "I need four or five full hours of sleep."

"And you'll explain this to me later?"

"At breakfast."

Hall entered room 12 and undressed. He got into bed and left the light on. He had to fight off sleep. He had to make a grab at understanding what was going on. Now, or it might slide past him.

He'd seen Rivers at the Potomac Motel how many nights ago? One? Two? Three? No, four to be exact. And now Rivers was in Kinsale. How and why? How did Rivers go from being on the chase, behind him, to being ahead of him?

And then he couldn't fight the sleep anymore. He switched off the light and the Jameson black pulled him under. It was like stepping into a bottle of ink.

❧   ❧   ❧

It was late morning when he awoke. His eyes felt gritty and his tongue thick and rough. By the time he'd shaved and drawn a bath he could hear movement in Mac's room. The bath was hurried and uncomfortable. The tub had been built for people no taller than five-five.

Mac opened the door in his underwear. "Order me an American style breakfast. Lots of everything. I'll be there in five minutes."

The dining room was almost empty. There were two couples seated at different tables. English or Irish country squire types, tweedy and bulky with sweaters. To Hall's right, with her back to him, a woman was having breakfast alone. Something about the color of her hair, the shape of her back and shoulders, was lodged in his memory. Perhaps. Perhaps not. He headed toward her table. On the way, the kid with missing teeth who'd been with Hinson's son in the early hours moved to block his path.

"Sir …?" the waiter began.

"I think I see someone I know."

At the sound of his voice, Denise Lawton turned and looked over her shoulder. Yes, it was Denise, far away from the University of North Carolina and her political and Russian studies.

"May I join you?" Hall stopped behind the chair on Denise's left. "Or are you expecting Rivers?"

"Mr. Rivers is out for the moment."

"Does that mean I can sit with you?"

"Do."

Hall took his time over the breakfast menu. For himself a mixed grill and for Mac soft scrambled eggs, a rasher of bacon, toast and juice. Handing the menu to the waiter Hall said, "Mr. Macintosh will be joining us in a minute or two."

"Funny finding you here," Denise said.

"I laughed first," Hall said.

She was dressed in the American way. A dark wool skirt, a white sweater with beadwork down the front and knee length leather boots. "Mr. Rivers will be surprised to find you here."

"Is it still Mr. Rivers? I thought the relationship might have progressed beyond formality."

Mac stopped in the dining room doorway. He spotted Hall. Grinning, almost laughing to himself, he headed for the table.

Denise blushed. Or it was the flush of anger. "This is not a vacation. No matter what you think ..."

Mac dropped a huge hand on Hall's shoulder. "Hello, Willie. It looks like you're up to it again."

"This is Mac."

Mac executed a courtly bow.

"And this is Denise. I'm afraid I've forgotten her maiden name."

"It doesn't matter," Denise said.

The waiter, who'd gone into the kitchen when Mac arrived, returned with their breakfast plates.

With Mac at the table the atmosphere changed. Hall and Denise kept a polite balance while Mac chatted away, until Denise stared at him as if she couldn't decide whether he was the craziest man she'd ever met or the sanest.

They were over a second pot of coffee when Hall noticed that Mr. Hinson, their host, had entered the dining room. He seemed hurried, nervous, and he crossed the room at almost a gallop. He came to a stop directly behind Denise. "Mrs. Hubbard?" His voice was low and respectful. "Mrs. Hubbard?"

Hall tapped Denise on the arm. "That's you, dear."

Denise looked over her shoulder. "Yes?"

"There's been an accident. Mr. Hubbard's been injured."

Denise pushed back her chair. Hinson caught it and moved it aside. "Where is he?"

"In his room. The injury was not serious and he was treated at hospital and brought here."

Mr. Hinson and Denise crossed the room, heads together. "What kind of accident?"

"I'm afraid the car went out of control and ..."

Hall signed his breakfast check. Mac left a small but adequate tip. He did not believe, as he said often, in spoiling the common man.

In the lobby Hall said, "How about a breath of air?"

"Fine with me." Mac led the way. They stepped outside and stood under a gray, overcast sky. A sprinkle of windblown rain tapped at them.

"There," Hall said. The black Mercedes was parked at the far end of the line. The windshield was smashed on the left side, the passenger side on the European drive cars. The hole was large and regular.

"Odd." Mac put a hand on the hood and leaned forward to examine the hole. "It looks almost manmade, doesn't it?"

Hall used a hand to wipe moisture from the unbroken part of the windshield. "That's it. See the seatback?"

There was a tear in the seat about shoulder high. It looked dark, wet, as if it had been scrubbed with a damp cloth.

"I'd say a rifle. That's my guess."

"That doesn't explain the shape of the break in the windscreen," Mac said.

"It does if you were trying to disguise the truth of what went through here. I'd say somebody gave it a few taps with a large stone."

"You think somebody tried to kill your Mr. Rivers?"

"He's not mine anymore." Hall turned when the door to The Keep opened behind them. Denise stood there, one hand shielding her face from the light rain. Hall backed away from the Mercedes. He took a handkerchief from his pocket and wiped his hands. Denise waited for them in the entranceway.

"He wants to see you."

"How is he?" Hall passed the handkerchief to Mac so he could wipe his hands as well.

"In pain."

"He always did have a low threshold," Hall said.

"Will you come?" Denise was at the edge of pleading.

"It's either that," Hall said "or stay out here and get rained on.

CHAPTER ELEVEN

The room smelled of adhesive tape, sterile gauze and antiseptic. The medical scents warred with Rivers' strong ripe tobacco and his cologne.

The bodyguard opened the door and let Denise pass. He turned and filled the doorway. His eyes were hard. "You two carrying?"

"Not even a nail file," Hall said.

"Let him in," Rivers said from back of the room. He sounded tasty.

"Just you," the bodyguard said.

"He's my lawyer." Hall indicated Mac.

"Who is he?" Rivers asked.

"A friend. Air Vice Marshall MacIntosh."

"Let them in, Aaron."

The bodyguard, Aaron backed away. Then Hall could see Rivers. He was propped up in a bed, bare to the waist. A bulky bandage formed a hump on Rivers' right shoulder. Already pale, untanned, now Rivers looked almost bloodless.

"Denny," Rivers said, "see about a pot of coffee for our guests."

"Denny" was a pet name for Denise. Hall knew that was part of the pattern with Rivers and his nieces.

Denise passed Hall on the way to the door. She was blushing and her eyes were lowered. The door closed behind her. Rivers said, "I understand you two were at The Keep when I had my accident."

"What accident?" Hall said.

"We were here," Mac said.

"Why *are* you here?" Rivers squirmed. There was a twitch of pain on his face. Then it was gone.

"Why are *you* here?" Hall said.

"You're a pair," Mac said. "Questions to answer questions."

"He's not the bloody police," Hall said.

Mac grinned at Hall. "I like the way you used <u>bloody</u>. It makes all the difference in the world. Now I'm on your side."

"Who made the try on you?" Hall stood on one side of the bed. Mac faced him from the other side.

"Aaron." The bodyguard pushed his way past Mac and got a bottle of medicine and a water glass from the night table. He leaned over Rivers and dropped two pills into his open mouth. He held the glass while Rivers washed them down. Aaron backed away. "A rock was thrown against the windshield by a truck in front of us."

"You sure it wasn't a boulder?" Mac said.

"Aaron didn't react well," Rivers said. "He braked and I was thrown against the dash."

"Careless of you," Hall said to Aaron.

Aaron drew his lips into a tight, angry line. He didn't answer.

"Is there someone else in your party?" Rivers said.

"We're it," Mac said.

"No contacts here? No wild Irish boys from across the north border?"

"Not a one," Mac said.

"Curious," Rivers said.

There was a tap on the door. Denise entered, followed by the waiter from the dining room. He carried a huge tray on his shoulder. On it there was a brightly decorated coffee pot. Talk stopped while the waiter arranged cups and saucers and a sugar dish and a creamer. Aaron saw him to the door and closed it behind him.

"All that talk about contacts and wild Irish boys," Hall said. "You think I'm hunting you? The last I heard you were hunting me."

"A fox will sometimes turn and run under the horses of the hunters. It is a way of confusing the scent."

"Does it work?"

"It works unless one of the horses steps on the fox." Rivers seemed pleased with his metaphor. He took half a cup of coffee when Denise offered it and drank with his free hand. He didn't use a saucer. "How do you happen to be here, Will?"

Hall told a careful story. He had to protect Franklin. In his new version, the boy ninja had lived long enough to give him a name and an address on Tedworth Square in London. With that, and with Mac's help, Hall traced Boyle that far and from there to Kinsale. The Keep address was on a receipt in Boyle's room. He'd visited Kinsale two days before he flew to New York on his way to Washington and the try on Hall.

"Any truth in this?" The question was directed at Mac.

"Close," Mac said. "He left out the fact that we had some help from a man at I branch."

"Your influence reaches that far, Mr. Macintosh?"

"Old debts, old favors," Mac said. "It might even reach into Ireland."

"Denny," Rivers said, "I think the Air Vice Marshal is trying to run a scam on us."

Denise looked at Mac. "I have a feeling it's true."

"Is it true, Will?"

"My experience is that Mac has friends and IOUs spread all across Europe."

"I'll run a dossier on you the next free time I have."

"Flattery," Mac said. "I'm retired now."

"Who took the potshot at you, Rivers?"

Rivers turned his head and stared at Hall. For an instant, denial was on the edge of his tongue. He swallowed that and said, "I thought at the time it might be you. That the fox might have grown some claws."

Hall shook his head.

"Someone working with you?"

"If I get tired of the chase, I'll do it myself. You were out early today, Rivers."

"I had a call from town."

"Anyone you know?"

"A man I didn't know said, for a sum, he would tell me what you were doing here in Kinsale."

"You talk to him?"

"He didn't show. On the way back, I got this." Rivers gestured toward his wounded shoulder.

"Your first Purple Heart?"

Rivers' eyes fluttered. The painkiller was making him sleepy. "Let's talk later. Denny will fill you in on what we're doing here."

Aaron closed the door behind them. Mac stood behind Denise. He lifted his eyebrows in a question.

"Why don't you take a rest, Mac? I'll talk to you later."

Mac lowered his right eyelid in a lazy wink. "Take her for a walk in the garden," he said.

It was a fair attempt at a formal garden, about half an acre of grass and hedges. In the spring, when the flowers bloomed and the grass was green, it might have been a pleasant walk. Now there was a tint of dull brown to it. Off to the side there was a screened-in pen where gold-necked pheasant strutted and preened.

"Denny is a nice nickname," Hall said.

"Yes." Her head was down and the toes of her boots kicked at the wet grass. "I'm only here to tell you what Mr. Rivers wants you to know."

"Do you have a pet name for him?"

Her voice hard and flat: "Not during office hours."

Hall backed away from it. "Will what Rivers want me to know be the truth?"

"The truth as we know it," Denise said. "Do you really hate Mr. Rivers?"

"In the general way I hate mumps and small pox."

"Do you trust him, Will?"

"Not a bit. He'd sell his mother or he already has." There was a noise at the cage. A pheasant was beating his wings and his chest at the wire. "What do you know about him?"

"Not much." Denise turned and looked at the screened-in cage. The pheasant who'd been trying to escape backed away and trembled and shook with rage or frustration.

"Ever hear of Beau Rivers? Dudley Rivers?"

Denise shook her head.

"Then you're not a sports fan. Beau and Dudley were older brothers to our Rivers up there." A thumb indicated the back of the Keep and the second floor. "Much older brothers. Both famous athletes. Football and track and basketball in a time when a man could letter in four sports if he wanted to. Beau was at Princeton and Dudley at Harvard. Both were household names for their time. Media stars. And then, years later, came our Mr. Rivers. Probably a late child, an accident when his mother considered herself safely beyond such concerns as motherhood. A weakling, a sickly child. In another time … or in our time if his mother had allowed it, he might have been drowned in the bathtub. His father did not like weakness. At any rate, he grew up somehow and went off to college. Not to Princeton or Harvard. To Yale. He couldn't hear the comparisons to Beau and Dudley. He had four scholarly years at Yale. But he wasn't to know the power of knocking heads the way Dudley and Beau had. So, he went after power in other ways. His bloodline demanded that. And, in time, he found that power in global chess games. Throw away two or three pawns here and catch a knight there. In global chess, none of the pawns bleed."

"Mr. Rivers bled."

"Not real blood," Hall said.

Denise shook her head, impatient with him. "I think he needs your help now."

"You're joking." He stared at her face and realized that she was serious. "He needs my help when he's got all the resources of the Company?"

Denise looked past him, at the rear of the Keep, the walls, the gray fitted stones and the mortar. "You know what The Keep really is?"

"A fancy, expensive hotel."

"That and a bit more. It's the site for a number of yearly company retreats. Not our Company. Business companies. It's private. All twelve rooms can be booked at one time. Mr. Hinson, the host, is discreet. The Keep is booked about six months a year, a week at a time, by some of the biggest organizations in the world. The check River did on Boyle, the man you killed in Washington, brought him here by a different route. The Company found a notebook in Boyle's room in Washington. A travel journal, of sorts. Of course, there were no notes of a business kind. That would have been dangerous. What he described were the hotels, the food, the countryside. There's even a semi-illiterate description of the gold-necked pheasant in these cages. The name of the hotel, The Keep, rang a bell somewhere in Rivers. He decided it was worth a deep check."

"What did he remember?"

"That a secret meeting of a few select members of OPEC took place here once. That was before the full meeting in Paris. It was probably a strategy session behind closed doors."

Hall remembered that the same paper had crossed his desk in Costa Verde. It hadn't, he thought, meant anything to him at the time. Movement caught his eye. At the second-floor window, Aaron was watching them.

"Two weeks ago, at the time Boyle was visiting The Keep, the other eleven rooms were taken by Worldwide Metals. Do you know of them?"

"No."

"A cartel. Through its member companies it controls almost seventy percent of the world's metals, the raw materials. Would you like to know a company that controls another ten percent?"

"You'll tell me."

"United Mining, Limited," Denise said.

The company that owns Costa Verde. The Lear jet that flew the Team from Costa Verde after the murder of Marcos had been owned by United."

"United was not represented at the meeting here at The Keep. It appears, from Company research, that a war is being fought between Worldwide and United. In the past, it was waged in the stock markets. Only recently it has progressed to the political arena as well."

"Costa Verde."

"Now you've got it, big boy."

"And the Company was caught in the middle?"

Denise gave him a short, positive nod. "You were one of their pawns, if you'd like to talk some more about pawns."

A thought, a dim possibility. "Paul Marcos?"

Denise smiled. "I wondered how long it would take you. Yes, your friend, Marcos. The moderate party. Worldwide had them in their hip pocket. The problem Marcos had was that United had us, the Company, in their hip pocket."

"Choices," Hall said, "choices."

"If Marcos had been elected in Costa Verde, it might have meant a shifting of another three percent of the world's raw materials to Worldwide. Seventy-three percent is always better than seventy percent. The moderate party and Marcos would have nationalized the mines and then turned around and made their deal with Worldwide. Will, you were taken by a pretty face and what Mr. Rivers would call too much optimism about the human animal."

"Marcos was a pretty face, wasn't he?" Hall said.

Aaron continued to watch them from the second level window of The Keep.

"The death of Marcos and the suspension of the promised free elections in Costa Verde meant that Worldwide had lost out. What we think happened then was that Worldwide decided to find a way to discredit United. At the same time, it's an odd way of thanking you for your support of their man. They hatch a plot and they use you again. The first step is the article written by the disenchanted ex-field man. The expose of the Company's work in Costa Verde and their involvement in the death of Marcos."

"But United isn't mentioned in the article," Hall said.

"That's too pat." Denise said. "United's part in the Costa Verdean political tangle would have been revealed in step two. At least that's what Mr. Rivers believes. What starts out to be an expose of the Company's ruthlessness in Costa Verde would have been followed by a second article or a series of letters to *The Truth Seeker* that would chart United's dirty hands in the matter."

"Wheels within wheels."

"You're thinking about Winford Boyle," Denise said.

"About to," Hall said. "Worldwide hires Boyle to waste me before the article comes out. Either I'm stirring up too much water, or they want to use my death to blacken the Company and through them to discredit United once more."

"Can you imagine what *The Washington Post* would do when they made the connection? At first your death and the death of your friend…"

"Bilbo."

"…would be listed as murder committed during a robbery. Then *The Truth Seeker* article appears. It wouldn't take a genius at *The Washington Post* to make the tie-up. Ex-Company man writes article and dies a violent death, just before the article is published."

"And there's a second result if Boyle had been lucky. I wouldn't be around to deny I wrote the article."

"You're convinced now?"

"I suppose I am," Hall said.

They moved away from the pheasant pen and walked along the path in the formal garden. Aaron moved away from the window high above them.

"After he's rested, Mr. Rivers will want to talk to you."

"Denny, huh? He calls you that?"

"This morning was the first time." Denise stepped around him and faced him in the path. "I think it's his way of getting back at you."

"How would that bother me?"

"He had an exaggerated idea that there was something going on between us," Denise said.

"Does he now?"

"Yes." Eyes level, meeting his. "Absurd, isn't it? He knows I sleep with anybody the Company tells me to sleep with."

"How many men has that been?"

"You want a list? I'll have to sit down with a pen and paper. It might take an hour to remember all of them."

Hall caught her wrist. "Just a ballpark figure."

She tried to pull her hand away. "I don't remember. As I said I need..."

"A hundred? Less than a hundred?"

"You're hurting me."

"Fifty? Less than fifty?"

"Hurt me if it makes you feel better."

"Twenty? Less than twenty?"

"One. And I didn't have to sleep with you if I hadn't wanted to." She freed her hand and marched away from him.

Five minutes later, damp from the light windblown rain, Hall entered the hotel. Hinson, the host, was behind the desk.

"The Air Vice Marshal is waiting for you in the bar." Hinson led the way.

The Guinness was cool and thick and dark. Mac passed a pint to Hall and sat down across the table from him.

"One thing about Guinness," Mac said. "It doesn't travel well."

Hall sipped his pint. It was as smooth as cream.

"A sea voyage spoils it." Mac said.

"A perfect reason to visit Ireland," Hall said.

"It was a long talk you had with the girl."

"It was, wasn't it?" Hall hadn't decided how much to tell Mac. "I think I've been three or four kinds of a fool with the girl."

"One kind of fool is enough," Mac lifted his pint. After he drank, he said, "The business with Rivers, is it working out?"

"Maybe. At least, now there's a good guess about what's going on. From this point on, I think you'd better stay outside. In fact, I think you ought to return to London or Kent."

"Used and cast aside?"

"Think of it as a perspective godfather's gift to the expected godchild. A living father. I have a feeling this is going to be rough."

"Mr. Hall." Denise stood in the doorway. Her voice was tight. "Mr. Rivers want to see you now."

Hall turned to Mac, who said, "I'll see about getting the next ferry to Wales."

"It might be the best thing." Hall stood and put out his hand. "Until the next time."

Mac grinned. "It's due in five or six months."

"The boy?"

"The christening," Mac said.

CHAPTER TWELVE

Within an hour, the British SAS Westland Commando helicopter landed in a clearing across the road from The Keep. It was accompanied by a Westland Lynx cover ship flying shotgun above and directly behind the Commando. The Lynx darted side- to-side, hovering, while Aaron and Hall loaded Rivers on board. With the four passengers seated and the door closed, the Commando headed for Shannon.

An 833A Viking had been dispatched from a U.S. carrier off the coast. It waited, a Navy doctor aboard, on an apron in the military berthing area.

While Rivers was taken aboard, Hall stood on the apron and watched the Lynx, a G.E. minigun mounted in the doorway, moving, covering, wheeling side-to-side while the Commando disembarked its passengers. Then the Commando whirred upward and away, trailed by the Lynx. The helicopters vanished beyond a tangle of hangers.

The Warden, Edgar Moss, met them at the former safehouse in the Virginia countryside. The colonial home was on twenty-five acres of land. The estate had been used to house defectors until the Director decided, because of one aborted escape attempt, that the location had been compromised. Now the house was kept on the books as a Company recreational center, until such a time when it could be sold and another safehouse purchased to replace it.

Two male nurses wheeled Rivers into the first-floor bedroom. Moss, heavy and pink-skinned as a baby, met Hall and Denise and offered them the use of the bar while Rivers was being prepared for the conference. Denise said she'd like a glass of white wine. Hall found a chilled bottle in the refrigerator under the bar and drew the cork. After he poured a glass for her, he mixed a scotch and water for himself. All the time he was aware that Moss was staring at him.

The Warden was chief of internal security for the Company. As such, he was Rivers' direct superior. The dogs let loose on Hall, that could not have been done without an okay from Moss.

"To the safe return," Moss said. "Ireland appears to be a murderous place these days."

"Dangerous to strangers," Hall said.

"A swimmer from the ferry you were on and then the try on Rivers."

"Washington is as bad," Hall said.

"Boyle?" The Warden nodded. A vain man, Moss combed his thin hair across the bald center of his head. "I think we have been running at cross purposes."

Denise sipped her wine, ankles crossed demurely and her eyelids lowered when she looked at Hall. *One*, she'd said in the formal garden behind The Keep. *Only one*.

The bedroom door opened and the gantry was wheeled outside by the two male nurses. After a few moments, Aaron stood in the doorway. "I think he's comfortable enough to talk now."

"Bring a drink with you," Moss said to Hall. He looked at Denise and hesitated. "I'm not sure whether we need you, Miss Lawton. Perhaps you'd like a bath and a rest. Aaron will find you a room…"

"I thought Denise might work with me on this," Hall said. "That is, if I'm going to work with you…"

"Fine with me." The Warden found the bottle of white wine and poured a trickle into Denise's glass. While Moss poured, his back was to Hall. Hall watched Denise's eyes open wide, seeing him for the first time since the walk in the formal garden. "Ready?"

Aaron backed away from the doorway and turned aside.

"I see it this way." Rivers held up a pal and shaky finger. "One. There is a matter of some housecleaning at the Farm. In this whole screw-up, the opposition has been half a step behind us or half a step ahead."

"A leak," The Warden said.

"Worldwide Metals…and I am certain they are behind this…has ears somewhere in the middle of the circuit."

"Where?" Moss tipped cigarette ashes into the palm of his hand until Aaron brought him an ashtray.

"I think we can construct compartments," Rivers said. "A way of slicing the circuit into airtight parts so that we can feed some quite different information in and see which version surfaces at Worldwide."

"You have a plan?" The Warden leaned forward and flicked an ash from the shiny toe of his black Chuka boot.

"There's a touch or two to add. I'll have it by morning if I'm not too drugged to do the thinking."

"Take all the time you need. Aaron will stay with you and give you the shot when the plan's solid."

"By morning then." Rivers took up a tumbler of water and drank with a glass straw. "Two. What are we going to do about Worldwide?"

"That's the hard one." Moss shook his head. "It might take years and a large part of our resources if we attempted a Wall Street operation."

"Self-defeating," Rivers agreed.

"Still, they've tried to use us. That is what is hard to forgive."

"There is no question of forgiveness," Rivers said. "We need to give them a warning. A spectacular warning."

"A bruise that won't go away for a year." Moss nodded.

Hall finished his drink. He turned and held the empty glass toward Aaron. "Scotch, water and two ice cubes."

Aaron hesitated. His eyes darted toward Rivers. Rivers nodded and Aaron took the glass and left the room.

"I have an idea that might serve as a beginning," Hall said. "The article in *The Truth Seeker* was the first move in the game. Do you have any plan to block publication of this issue?"

"I'm afraid we can't." The Warden shrugged. "Unless we decide to torch the printing plant in Newark."

"Then the article will appear?"

"I'm afraid so. Of course, we will refuse to comment on the specific details."

"Enos Blackman refused to believe I hadn't written the article. He may be willing to add a box. New, additional information."

"I don't follow you," Moss said.

Hall told him.

The Warden put back his head and laughed. Even Rivers smiled.

"I'll need some information, the proof that establishes Worldwide's connection with Paul Marcos and the moderate party."

The Warden swallowed the laugh. "I can do better than that. I can have the box written and delivered here by morning."

"I'll fly to New York tomorrow for a meeting with Blackman."

"Fine." Moss seemed pleased.

"I'd like to take Miss Lawton with me," Hall said. "To watch my back."

The Warden said, "Why not?"

The Warden broke up the meeting.

❧   ❧   ❧

In the night. A raw wind blew through the trees outside the bedroom where Will Hall slept and awoke and slept again. The curtains were open and he could see the dark night sky. In a way he wished for snow, for the pale flutter and fall. For the peace of snow. For that sense.

He was half awake when the air pressure in the room changed. It was almost impossible to detect but he felt it. The door had opened and then closed. He braced himself. There was only a one in a hundred chance that the security at the safehouse had been penetrated.

A count of ten, waiting. Then he relaxed. He could smell her perfume. She crossed the room on bare feet and stopped at the side of the bed.

"I don't blame you for what you said to me in the garden. You have a right to be bitter and distrusting. I would be if I were in your position," Denise said. "I want to make things clear."

The robe she wore was too large for her. Probably a man's, furnished from the stock they kept at the safehouse for foreign visitors.

"Okay," Hall said.

"I'm here because I want to be. That's the way it was before. And that's the way it is now."

Denise opened the robe, removed it and dropped into the seat of a chair behind her. When she turned back toward the bed, she was wide-legged. Hall lifted a hand and touched her on the inside of her thigh. The skin there was incredibly soft.

"Do you believe me?" she asked.

Hall did. "I'm getting there."

Teasing, she edged forward until his hand was trapped, caught between her thighs. "What can I do to convince you?"

He moved his free hand and wrapped the arm around her. He pulled her forward, tumbling her over him and partly on top of him.

"We'll think of something," he said.

Hall made two phone calls from the airport. The first was to George, the doorman at his uncle's apartment on Riverside Drive. The apartment was not being used.

The second call was to Enos Blackman at the magazine office.

"Mr. Hall, I think we have had our conversation. I think I've told you that I have no intention ..."

"Wait a minute. Since I saw you some new information has come into my hands. It doesn't change anything in the original article. It does, however, enlarge upon what was really happening in Costa Verde."

"I can see you at twelve-fifteen," Blackman said.

"It's a love nest." Hall emptied his suit bag and pushed the hangers to one side of the bedroom closet. "The other half is yours."

"Half the apartment?" Denise was smiling.

"And half the bed as well."

Denise sat on the edge of the bed. "So, you have a fancy love nest in New York?"

"It seems so."

"A summer house in Blowing Rock. A love nest in New York. Anything else?"

"A flat in London."

"I heard you were wealthy." Denise tapped the toe of her shoe against the floor, the sound muffled by the carpet. "I think that was when I decided to set my cap for you."

"A quaint expression for a modern girl." Hall striped away his tie and removed his shirt. He found a soft gray wool turtleneck in a dresser that held some of his belongings. He pulled the sweater over his head and adjusted the shoulders. "The truth is that the big money is on the other side of the family. An uncle on the Harker side of the family leases this apartment and the flat in London. Poor relations are allowed the use when he's not in town."

"And the house in Blowing Rock, the one you didn't invite me to?"

"That's mine, as long as I can pay the taxes."

Denise smiled. "At least you're almost a third as wealthy as I imagined you were."

Hall found a topcoat in a storage bag. He struggled into it and wrapped a scarf around his throat. Denise followed him to the door that led to the hallway.

"How do you want to play this?"

"You get to Blackman's building ahead of me. I'll be at a phone booth a block or so away. Walk past the building, see if you can spot surveillance or anything that seems out-of-place. If it looks clear, call me at the phone booth." Hall said. "I'll go in and see Blackman. You keep watch outside. Before I leave, I'll look out the window. If there's trouble, have a newspaper in your hand or under your arm. If it's all clear, don't have anything."

"Seems simple enough."

It wasn't brilliant trade craft, but sometimes it was the simple approach that worked best.

The incredibly thin girl led Hall through the maze of desks and stopped at Enos Blackman's doorway "He's here."

"Come in, Mr. Hall."

Hall entered the office and remained standing. Behind him the girl said, "I'm going to the deli to get lunch."

"Lean corned beef on seeded rye, potato salad and a pickle."

"To drink?" the girl said.

"Cream soda." Enos passed a five-dollar bill to the girl and then closed the door after she moved away. He turned and motioned Hall to a chair. He sat behind the desk and placed his elbows on the desk blotter. "I was afraid when you called it was another ..."

"No reason for you to think otherwise." Hall pulled the plain brown envelope from his topcoat pocket and passed it across the desk. While Blackman read the two typed pages, Hall removed his topcoat and folded it over the back of his chair.

At the safehouse, earlier in the morning, he'd checked over the "new, additional information" that Moss had supplied him. What the paper did was document Worldwide Metals' ties to Paul Marcos and the moderate party in Costa Verde. What had been, in the article that *The Truth Seeker* was publishing, a one-sided matter, the Company and the right wing against a legitimate political party now became a war between two large multinational companies.

Overall, it could have been his writing, his voice, but he'd taken the time to change a word here and there, striking out a word he wouldn't use and substituting one that he would.

Across the desk, Enos Blackman read the two typed pages once. He closed his eyes for a long moment. When he opened his eyes, he nodded to himself and re-read the paper. "It's worse than I thought," he said finally.

"They don't really fight over bananas anymore."

"Sharks trying to swallow other sharks," Blackman said. He tapped the two pages. "It's a better story, your article with this added to it. More balanced."

"My thought exactly," Hall said.

"Only there's a problem," Blackman said. "The paste-up's done. I don't know where we can add this." Blackman opened a desk drawer on his right and brought out the paste-up, the model, for the new issue. The cover was in gray with a black border. The banner, across the top, was in black as well. Centered below the banner was the main article of the issue.

THE COMPANY STRIKES AGAIN IN COSTA VERDE
William K. Hall

Hall put out a hand. Blackman passed the paste-up to him. Hall took a few minutes to flip through the magazine. It was full, every space taken. Hall turned it in his hands. He was about to return the mock-up to Blackman. He stopped when he saw the blank back of the cover. "Anything here?"

"No, we never…" Blackman turned the back cover toward him. "It might fit. I think it will, even if we have to drop down a type face size or two."

The outside door opened and closed. The thin girl knocked and entered. She placed a paper bag and Blackman's change on the corner of the desk She was backing toward the doorway when Blackman stopped her. "Sheila, after you've had your sandwich, I need you."

Hall stood and put on his topcoat. "I guess that's all."

Blackman smiled and put out his hand. "No charge for this?"

Hall glanced out the window. Denise pretended to be window shopping across the street. There was no newspaper in her hands. All clear.

"Not a penny," Hall said.

CHAPTER THIRTEEN

Rivers hadn't allowed them to transport him to the hospital. A doctor, with a military bearing but wearing a suit, was leaving when the Company car delivered Denise and Hall to the safehouse. The doctor tossed his black medical bag into the passenger side of his new black BMW and stood looking back at the safehouse, shaking his head.

The Warden was in the living room drinking coffee. Hall took the coffee Moss offered. Denise said she was tired and carried her bag upstairs to her room. Hall nodded at the closed bedroom door. "How's the second in command?"

"He's being stubborn. I've been trying to get him to the hospital all day."

"That's the Beau Rivers syndrome."

"Huh?" Moss blinked at him.

"His brother, Beau, played the second half of the Princeton-Yale game one year with a broken arm. Just took a wide roll of adhesive tape and wrapped the arm."

"Hmmmm." Moss didn't appear to care for Hall's insight. He preferred to think that all the men in the Company had that inner toughness that a gentleman always had. "While you were in New York..." Hall thought Moss wanted to add "...enjoying yourself." "While you were there, Rivers worked out the details of the compartments."

He carried his cup to the coffee pot and fixed himself a refill. "Yes?"

"It's quite brilliant really. Rivers thought of the circuit in terms of three compartments. Each is divided by what we can think of as firewalls. A way of blocking access from one compartment into the others. Then we fed different information into each compartment."

"Did it work?"

"We'll know soon."

Hall gulped his coffee and put the cup aside. "Rivers want to see me?"

"He's resting now." Moss followed Hall to the foot of the staircase. "No trouble with Blackman?"

"It was like giving candy to a baby."

Hall went back to Denise's room. She was asleep on her bed, laying on her side in only her bra and panties. An afternoon nap. He moved onto the bed beside her, facing her back, and nuzzled her neck. He slipped his hand between her legs and stroked her very gently with his fingertips through the thin fabric of her underwear. After a time, her breathing changed and she awakened with a low moan, her eyes still closed.

"Am I dreaming?" she whispered.

"Is it a good dream?" he asked, sliding his hand up to her flat stomach.

"I'll let you know," she said and pushed his hand back down between her legs.

There was more color in Rivers' face. Aaron, on the other hand, looked pale and drained and red-eyed, as if he hadn't slept since Rivers was shot.

Hall stopped Moss in the doorway. He said, in a voice that didn't reach far beyond them, "I think Aaron needs a sleeping pill and about twenty hours sleep. I can take the afternoon turn at being a body keeper."

Moss was blind to a lot of what was going on around him. He pushed himself so much that he didn't recognize a worn-down co-worker unless it was pointed out to him. "I can do better than that. I can have another man here by this evening."

"Good idea."

Rivers had a fresh pillow placed behind his head. He almost seemed friendly. "I understand it went well in New York."

Hall nodded. "Blackman will run the new note. It opened his eyes, you might say. Now, to him, it's sharks trying to swallow other sharks."

"That's an improvement," River said.

Moss shifted in his chair. "I'm calling in another man. From the looks of him I'd say Aaron needs a vitamin shot and a few hours of sleep."

"Good of you to think of him."

"The least I can do." The Warden seemed pleased with himself.

Rivers lifted a hand and pressed the bandage on his shoulder. "Where's Denny? You leave her in New York?"

"She's fixing lunch."

"I hope she was helpful."

"Very," Hall said.

Rivers didn't press it. "I thought you might be interested in the way I've set up the compartments."

"If it's not too complicated for me to understand."

"The Warden handled it for me. Administration, operations and communications, those three compartments. Each of them received a different packet. Each with a standard initial slip. For example, the packet received at administration had already been initialed by operations and communications." Rivers allowed himself a sly grin. "No reason, therefore, for that packet to return to operations or communications, right? It was the same with the information delivered to operations. Already initialed by administration and communications. And on and on. You understand the concept?"

Hall dipped his head. "I'm more concerned with the kind of information you furnished them."

"Administration was told the truth, that you were back in the fold and vindicated to some degree. Operations was told that you were considered killed in Ireland, Communications was informed that you'd worked out the Marcos connection with Nationwide Metals."

"Any reaction?"

"Not yet," Rivers said.

"I guess we wait then."

Rivers nodded. "That's the program."

Hall led the way from the room. Before Moss pulled the door closed behind him, Hall saw Aaron feeding Rivers another pain pill.

It was early evening. Dusk wasn't very different from the overcast sky that had been there most of the day. A light, wet snow fell. It fluttered down on the hard snow crust that surrounded the safehouse.

Head down, an arm around Denise's shoulders, Hall picked his way through the trees. Now that he was, in effect, reinstated there was no problem about the Python .357 that he'd taken from Freddy Webb at his Blowing Rock house. The Warden was even forward enough to offered him a box of loads to replace the spent shells. The weight of the Python dragged at the right pocket of the parka. Not that he believed he would need it. As far as he could tell, the safehouse was just that, a safe place. However, The Warden, when Hall said that he and Denise were going for a walk, had suggested that he carry, just in case, The Warden had said that he'd like a walk himself but he was waiting for the relief bodyguard to spell Aaron for a day or so.

They stopped in a clearing. Beyond the clearing, as one boundary, there was a stream that was hardly more than a ditch. They'd walked slowly and they were, he estimated, about two hundred yards from the house. The water in the stream ran sluggishly, clogged with patches of ice. Hall stopped and looked down at the stream. He wasn't dressed for fording even a shallow stream.

Denise placed her back to the stream. "You don't seem taken with Rivers' plan."

"That's only part of it."

"What is?" Wet snow stuck to Denise's eyebrows.

Hall lifted a hand stroked the snow away. "I think he's trying to be too clever. He hasn't considered the risks. The crap about compartments. It's easier to talk about than to accomplish. Say Worldwide's got a man in one unit... operations. What's to keep him from having a cup of coffee with a man from communications? *Too bad about what happened to Hall, huh?* That's the man from operation who thinks I'm reported dead in Ireland. *What do you mean?* the man from communications says. *He's alive and well and probably somewhere in Virginia.* And then it's a simple matter to—"

There was a muffled crackling in the distance, from the direction of the safehouse.

It was the unmistakable sound of a submachine gun, Hall thought. Probably an Ingram with a noise suppressor

Denise's eye widened and her face paled. He nodded, acknowledging her thought, reached into his right parka pocket and brought away the Python .357. It couldn't match the firepower he'd heard.

Hall had seen the arms cabinet at the house. It was located in the kitchen next to the pantry. He'd had his look when he'd been getting loads for the .357. Two or three of the old standby, the .45

automatic, a Dan Wesson .357 with a six-inch barrel, an M-16 and an M-21 with a 3-9 Redfield scope. Those and boxes of loads and clips. But no Uzi and no Ingram.

There was another extended burst from the subgun. Hall wrapped his free arm around Denise. "Are you dressed warm enough?"

"I think so."

There was a large thick clump of bushes next to the stream. It was snow covered. Hall pulled her in that direction. "Under there," he said.

"I'll go with you."

"Not this time." He circled the bush and lifted a section of it. There was a cavity formed under it. A frightened bird, moving so that that Hall couldn't identify it, broke cover. One wing brushed Hall's shoulder. "In there." She dropped to her knees and crawled under the bush. "Stay here until I call you. Stay here until morning if you have to. If I don't come back at all, you head west until you reach the highway. You can probably hitch a ride."

She didn't argue.

Hall lowered the section of the bush. He thought he heard another burst from the subgun. Working hurriedly, he scooped snow from a low mound and threw it about until he had covered most of the tracks that led to the bush. It wasn't as good a job as he would have liked. Maybe it wouldn't matter. It was almost dark now and the slow fall of wet snow might complete the work. "Remember. Until morning if I don't come back for you."

"Be careful, Will." There was a shiver in her voice.

There was a silence in the distance now. He walked in the direction of that silence.

When he and Denise left the safehouse for the walk there had been a glow of light from inside. The porch light, twin spots, hadn't been lit. From his shadow place at the edge of the woods, Hall saw that it was changed around completely now. The house was dark and the twin spots blazed downward from the edge of the roof.

Hall remained beyond the reach of the lights. Still as the tree he stood beside. A dark form, a body, sprawled on the steps, face down. The body seemed wedged there, like a fly that had been swatted and mashed into place. From the bulk, Hall guessed that it was Aaron. There was no movement and no sound.

No reason to be careless, Hall told himself.

He backed away from the light and followed the woods that ran parallel to the narrow road that led from the highway to the safehouse. Halfway to the highway, there was a scraped area to one side. Parking spaces for five or six cars. Earlier in the day, two cars had been parked there, a black Mercedes that belonged to Rivers and the Company car, a tan and white Ford station wagon. The same now, he told himself. The same two cars. But there was the smell, the hint, of exhaust in the cold clean air. Hall started across the road and stopped. New tracks, heavy snow tires, were printed in the snow crust, each detail clear and clean, unspoiled by the slow snow flutter.

He trotted south, toward the stream. He'd cut the angle too sharp and missed the bush. He followed the stream until he found it. "Denise?"

There was a rustle, scratching, and Denise clawed her way from under the bush. She ran against him, her arms circling his neck. "I was worried. What happened?"

Her hands were cold. He shoved the Python into his pocket and broke the clasp at his neck. He held her hands between his until they felt warmed.

"I don't know yet. I had to be sure they were gone, whoever they were. It looks like a strike of some kind. But I couldn't leave you out here while I checked."

"Any survivors?"

He knew of at least one likely casualty. "Let's go find out."

Before they stepped into the patch of light from the twin spots, Hall lifted the Python and held it at the ready. He put his left arm around Denise and guided her to the other side of the steps, past Aaron's body to the doorway.

"Don't look back," he said. He left her and moved down the stairs and squatted next to Aaron. First, he noticed that Aaron was wearing a tweed jacket, no outer coat. That probably meant he'd stepped outside with the expectation that the time away from the warmth would be brief. Hall leaned down and caught Aaron by one shoulder. He pulled him upward, long enough to see the damage that the Ingram or whatever it was had done to Aaron's chest and stomach. A burst of twenty rounds or so had almost torn Aaron in half. Hall released the dead man's shoulder. No heartbeat, no pulse. He'd probably been dead about the time he hit the steps.

"It's going to be ugly in there," Hall said to Denise, who had her back to him and Aaron. She didn't want to see it. "Prepare yourself."

Hall opened the door and stepped inside. Denise followed him, one hand on his arm. He touched the light switch to the right of the doorway. The overhead lights flared on. He'd prepared himself for more blood. The living room was empty. Hall turned and caught Denise by the hand

The door to the bedroom was ajar. Hall went in that direction, Denise stayed behind. A push at the door and he stopped in the doorway. There was light in the room from an overturned lamp. Rivers had tried to roll out of bed. He'd had trouble. Now he was frozen in place, his feet trapped in the sheets and blankets. The top half of his body hanging over the side of the bed. A stitch of rounds from the subgun had walked its way up his spine and blown off the top of his head.

Hall backed from the bedroom. He closed the door until he was the way it had been. Denise stared at him. Hall shook his head. "Rivers, too."

That left Moss, The Warden. Hall pictured the scenario.

Aaron goes outside for some reason. Is hit there. Moss hears the subgun. What does Moss do? Even if he is carrying a handgun, he knows he is outgunned. What does he do? What would I do?

"Wait here," Hall told Denise.

He found Moss at the arms cabinet beside the kitchen pantry. The doors unlocked, probably reaching for the M-16. A clip on the floor beside him. The wood of the right door to the arms cabinet splintered. The subgunner walking the rounds right to left, low to high, hitting Moss in the hip and spinning him. Then in the chest as he turned. The head shot when Moss was down. Brain tissue splattered across the floor and the baseboards.

Hall returned to the living room. He found a decanter of cognac in the liquor cabinet. He poured two heavy shots. He handed one to Denise and watched her sip. He gulped his. His stomach flipped. He was queasy.

"It was a sweep," he said.

He poured another shot for himself and carried it to the phone. He dialed the Farm number.

"This is Hall. Delta two, delta four, Bravo one, fox three."

The story told. His story recounted in one of the upstairs bedrooms while Denise was questioned in a room down the hall. During this time, the cleanup was going on in the kitchen, the first-floor bedroom and the front steps.

While he talked, Hall drank mugs of hot coffee. His nerves were better now, he thought, and he considered the problem housekeeping had. The weather too nasty for a sailing accident. Who'd be out in this kind of mess? No, it would be a skid on bad roads. Aaron driving and Rivers and Moss passengers in the back seat Not just a crash. A fire as well. Midnight or later when the roads were clear of some of the usual traffic. Too bad about Rivers' black Mercedes.

"You'll take a polygraph?" Ray Stiggers asked.

"Any time you want," Hall said.

Two men were in the room with Hall. One was a bone-breaker. Hardly a word from him the whole time. He was in the room to be sure that Hall didn't try to do something that wasn't planned for. The second man, Ray Stiggers, the one doing the questioning, he was the interesting one. Out of Brown the same year Hall left Yale. He was the number three man in security. Said to be a Rivers' apprentice. Stiggers had some of the same mannerisms as his mentor. The pipe, the harsh tobacco and the English tailoring. Any similarity ended there. The body under this tweed suit wasn't sickly. It was hard and flat as rolled steel. He was a tall man, with dark hair and a faint feathering of gray at the sideburns.

"Tonight?" Stiggers said.

"Fine with me. If being tired and strung out won't screw up the machine."

Stiggers shook his head. "Not likely." He took the warm pipe from his mouth and rubbed the bowl against the side of his nose, oiling it. Not, Hall thought, the kind of gesture Rivers would have made. Stiggers closed his notebook. "Too bad the girl was with you. Otherwise…"

"If she hadn't been out walking with me, she'd be zipped in a body bag by now. And, if I can guess the second part of the statement, I'd say you're out of your mind. If I hadn't had to hide Denise, I might have got back to the house and got a look at the killer or killers. But I'm not going up against an Uzi or an Ingram with a handgun. Not unless I've got a sure back shot at three or four feet."

Ray Stiggers want to avoid the putdown. "Killers?"

"Had to be at least two. It was a matter of timing." Hall stopped. "You want my guess?"

Stiggers nodded and rubbed the nose oil into the pipe bowl with his fingers. He clamped the pipe in his teeth.

"I'd say at least two men. Probably a driver who waited at the parking area. Somehow, they got Aaron on the porch. He was always armed but he wasn't carrying a weapon in his hands. Maybe he knew them. One man cut down on Aaron. That cleared the way to the door. The second man made his sprint for the entrance to the house. The first man probably made sure Aaron was out of it for good. Then he followed man number two. Probably about a step behind him. Moss was in the living room. He heard the sub-gun and knew he was outmanned. He made a run for the arms cabinet. Moss might have made it if there was only one killer."

Hall paused. "I didn't get a good look at the bedroom where Rivers was. Was he armed?"

Stiggers nodded. "Sidearm on the floor. Night table drawer partly open. Pistol probably was there and Rivers had trouble turning and reaching into the drawer. Before he could turn with the handgun, he caught it in the back."

"Two men," Hall said. "One man reached the living room in time to see Moss heading for the gun cabinet. That man followed Moss and got him before he could put a clip on the M-16. Fast work. Good timing with this team. A ten second delay, even less, and Moss would have been a dangerous man. Killer number one, the man who'd gunned Aaron, made his run for the first-floor bedroom. The same man couldn't have killed Moss and Rivers. Too little time. Rivers would have been armed. He might have got off a round or two. Rivers would have been prepared if he'd had the time it took the killer to finish off Moss. Moss would have been prepared if a single killer had finished off Rivers before coming after him."

"At least two men then," Stiggers said. "Too bad you didn't get a look at them."

"That bothers me," Hall said. "You know what else worries me?"

Stiggers talked around the pipe mouthpiece. "No."

"They didn't come looking for me."

Stiggers closed his eyes and sucked at the pipe.

Hall wasn't hungry. Denise insisted that they needed at least a bowl of soup. Stiggers and the other were in the living room, waiting for the polygraph machine and the operator to arrive from The Farm. Denise found two cans of black bean soup on a shelf above the stove. While the soup heated, she placed bowls on the table and told Hall to make himself useful.

"I need sherry and crackers," she said.

The weapons cabinet was closed but not locked. Hall passed it and stepped into the pantry. He flipped on the overhead light. There was a section of cradled wines and he read labels until he found a bottle of dry California sherry. He tucked the wine under one arm. Crackers? Crackers? Yes, there. A large tin of English water biscuits. He'd turned and started from the pantry when he heard the squeak. He stopped and waited. Another squeak. It was a familiar sound but he couldn't place it. He walked the length of the pantry, ears close to the shelves, until he located the source of the sound. *There.* What looked like the front of an antique flour bin. He pulled the front of the bin downward and leaned forward.

The tape recorder was still running. The squeak was at the head of the recorder. Probably needed cleaning or lubrication. The sound, that was where he'd heard it before.

On his way through the kitchen, he placed the sherry and the water biscuits on the counter. Denise said, "Aren't you going to pull the cork?"

Hall shook his head and went looking for Ray Stiggers.

❧   ❧   ❧

The kitchen smelled of the earthy black bean soup and the dollop of sherry had added to it. She ladled two bowls and when Stiggers looked hungrily at their supper she poured the remainder into another bowl and scraped the pot.

Stiggers thanked her.

On the other side of the kitchen, one of the bonebreakers set up the tape player. He'd found it in an equipment room in the attic.

It had taken Stiggers only a couple of minutes to find the trip switch for the recorder. It was concealed under the left arm of the stuffed chair that Moss usually sat in in the living room. There was an ashtray stand beside that chair, in it the dead half of one of the Cuban cigars the Warden smoked.

Stiggers showed Hall the switch. One touch and the recorder in the pantry stopped. On the way to the kitchen, Stiggers asked, "was there anything going on earlier that Moss might have wanted taped?"

"Not that I know about."

Now Stiggers spooned the black bean soup into his mouth and swallowed. "Bob," he said to the bonebreaker, "how much tape has run?"

"It's at the tail."

"Start it from the beginning."

Bob hit the play button. Hall was surprised to hear his voice at the start of the tape. "*No, I'll stay with the Colt Python. What I need is a fresh set of loads.*"

"*Help yourself,*" Moss said. "*That's Freddy's Python, isn't it?*

There was a loud rattling, what might have been rocks rolling around in a can. Hall knew it was his hand clawing through a box of .357 shells.

"*How long will you be gone?*"

The click of the .357's feeding into the cylinder. Hall said, "*Thirty or forty minutes. Denise and I need the air.*"

Sound of footsteps approaching. "*Ready, Will?*" Denise said.

"*And eager.*"

More steps. Down the hall to the living room. The front door opening and closing.

Aaron's voice: "*You trust him, Mr. Moss?*"

"*Yes.*" Moss said.

The tape went dead. "He switched it off at this point," Stiggers said.

Hall tilted his bowl and got the last spoonful of soup. "Why tape what we just heard?"

"Proof you had a weapon," Stiggers said. "It was like signing a chit you'd been issue a sidearm."

There was a loud noise from the tape. Moss was yelling.

"Cue it again," Stiggers said.

Bob reversed the tape. He hit play again. Moss said, "*Yes,*" to Aaron's question. Then the tape went dead.

"The first burst is here," Hall said. "The one that downed Aaron. That's when Moss hit the trip switch."

A loud noise.

"Somebody's kicking the front door in." Hall pushed his bowl aside and lifted his glass of white wine. He sipped and listened.

"*Jesus Lord,*" Moss shouted. It was almost a scream. "*Rivers, we're under attack.*" Footsteps. Moss running for the arms cabinet. Other footsteps mixed with the heavy panting from Moss. The cabinet doors opening and banging against the wall. The subgun, an Uzi or an Ingram, opens up and drowns out everything.

Almost immediately, before that reverberation fades, there is another sound in the first-floor bedroom. The door opening and a muffled voice said, "*Here's yours, Rivers.*"

The terrified voice of Rivers: "*No... bib... bib...*"

A long burst from the subgunner.

"What was he trying to say." Stiggers pointed the question toward Hall.

"It sounded like Bible."

"Run it again, Bob."

Bob ran it twice. It wasn't clear. "It does sound like Bible," Stiggers said.

On the tape hurrying footsteps, heavy breathing, almost panting. One voice: *"No sign of Hall."*

A second voice, muffled: *"We can't wait for him. Time's gone."*

Footsteps. Creaking of the door as it closes. Then silence on the tape.

"How long between the shooting and you return to the house, Hall?"

"Maybe ten minutes, give or take a minute."

Denise brought a second bottle of white wine from the refrigerator. Hall pulled the cork. Denise filled his glass, Stiggers' and her own.

"Bible?" Stiggers said. "That make any sense to you?"

"Not a bit."

"You recognize the voices?"

"Not the one that's clear. The man who killed Rivers was wearing something, a cloth or a scarf, over his mouth."

"Speed it up," Stiggers told Bob. "But don't miss anything."

Bob started and stopped his way through a long section of the tape. "Here." Bob backed the tape a foot or so and hit the play button again.

The door opening, footsteps. Hall said, *"Rivers, too."*

Denise lowered her head. Hall stood. "I've heard this before." He took Denise by the elbow and helped her to her feet. "Better if you get packed." He looked down at Stiggers. "Alright with you?"

Stiggers nodded.

When Hall returned to the kitchen a few minutes later, the tape was boxed and the player closed and ready to be stored away.

"Looks like you're clear of it," Stiggers said.

"Nice to know," Hall filled the sink with hot water and dish washing liquid. He rinsed the bowls and dropped them in the wash water.

"What?" Stiggers carried the wine glasses to the sink. He wet a cloth and wiped the kitchen table.

"Nothing."

"I heard you," Stiggers said. "Still pissed?"

"To the boiling point," Hall said.

CHAPTER FOURTEEN

It was approaching midnight. Denise's bags were packed and placed by the front door. Splinters around the lock, where the door had been kicked in, showed white against the dark stain of the door. Hall turned and looked at Denise and shook his head. "This isn't my idea."

"I know, Will."

"I think we've got time for a coffee." He took her elbow and turned her toward the kitchen.

Stiggers sat sprawled at the kitchen table. A Melita coffee-maker was on the stove, the filter draining in the sink. Hall sat Denise down across from Stiggers and got two cups from the cabinet. He filled both cups and placed one in front of Denise.

Ray Stiggers gulped his coffee. "It's a milk plane," he said to Denise. "It stops at Richmond and then at Raleigh-Durham."

Denise placed both hands around the coffee cup. She didn't drink. "I'd rather stay here."

"Admin gave the orders. It's not like I've got any say in it."

"The real question is whether I want to finish the program at the University. I'm not sure anymore." A rashness seemed to spur at her. She put her hand on Will's and looked at Stiggers. "I want to be where Will is."

"So, it's like that?" Stiggers smiled. "Perhaps you could wait for him there."

She glanced at Hall. "Where will he be?"

Stiggers shook his head. "That's for operations and security to decide."

"You're talking about me like I'm not here," Hall said.

"In some ways you're not," Stiggers said.

"Is he clear? Am I clear?"

"It's my estimate. It's all on the tape. I can't figure it any other way."

"Call it luck," Hall said. "We were lucky enough to be stomping around the countryside."

Bob, Stiggers' assistant, stopped in the doorway. "The car's ready to take Miss Lawton to the airport."

Denise tightened her grip on Hall's hand. "Now they're talking about me like I'm not here."

"It's the nature of the business," Hall stood and looked down at Stiggers. "One day you're here and the next you're not." He and Denise followed Bob to the living room.

Bob gathered up Denise's bags. "I'll put these in the boot."

Hall opened the door for him and closed it after he was outside. Hall put his arms around Denise. "Aren't we English around here? Boot? It must be the Rivers' influence."

Her breath was warm on his neck. "You'll call me when you can?"

"As soon as it's over."

Hall emptied Denise's cup and placed it in the sink. He reheated the coffee and topped off his cup. When he sat down next to Stiggers, he saw the black plastic briefcase that was on the table. Stiggers had his elbows on the briefcase.

"You knew what Rivers was trying to do? The plan he had about compartments?"

"I knew."

"What do you think happened with it?"

"You want an opinion?"

Stiggers nodded solemnly.

"Rivers out-cuted himself. All he really told admin and operations and communications was that he was playing games <u>and</u> that he was here at the safehouse."

"And ...?"

"It probably got him and Aaron and Moss killed."

"The tape ..."

"What about it?"

"One of the killers on the tape was asking about you," Stiggers said.

"Which means ...?"

"Operations was fed the information that you were considered killed in Ireland."

"That would clear operations if the compartments were really airtight, if the job came by way of the Company."

"That's the way Rivers would have seen it." Stiggers placed the briefcase on edge and unzipped it. "I was bringing this to Rivers. It landed on my desk late yesterday afternoon. The problem is I don't know how it fits in." He reached into the briefcase and brought out two sheets of paper. He read the first page, shook his head, and passed the pages to Hall.

It was a passport check for the man Mac tossed overboard on the ferry.

PP # M 2345085. Issued Salt Lake City, Utah to Baker, Warren Blair.

Issued: May 1977, ten-year limitation. Good until May 1987.

Purpose for use: business and vacation travel Intended visits: England, Ireland, France, Sweden and West Germany.

Hall lowered the page and looked at Stiggers. What he'd read didn't mean anything to him either. He read on.

Subject male born Boise, Idaho 1/12/1948. Enlisted army 7/8/68. Completed basic training, transferred to Special Forces. After advanced training assigned 2/14/69 Vietnam. Completed one tour. Volunteered 2nd tour. Discharged Fort Bragg, injury related, 40 percent disability, on 4/23/72

Two years with Denver Police Department. Night courses in criminology and police sciences on G.I. Bill, Left Denver Police Department 6/15/74. Reason for leaving: disciplinary action following charges of police brutality, beating of drunks in holding tank.

7/5/74 WW Security Services applied for status of investigator and security man for Baker, Warren Blair. Service with Special Forces and Denver Police Department noted in application. Omitted mention of charges against him by Denver Police Department. Status granted by state of Utah. Also permission to carry concealed arms. WW Security based Flat Canyon, Utah. •

Note: false statement possible in passport application. Subject male gave hometown as Copper City, Utah. No present town or city of that name in Utah atlas or abstracts. However, it was name of company mill town at the turn of the century. Site of International Workers of the World strike and riots 1910-11. Forty-three strikers killed before strike broken. Name, Copper City, changed 1932 to Flat Canyon.

"Can you make a call to someone at the research unit?"

"I think so," Stiggers said.

Hall passed him page two. "The riots and strikes mentioned here. What company was involved? Is that company still around?"

"The Wobs, huh?" Stiggers carried the page into the living room. Hall followed him. Stiggers drew the phone toward him and dialed the Farm number. "Stiggers," he said. "Fox three, Charlie one, alpha three, fox four." He waited, the time it took for the computer to check his identification. "Alright, patch me in with Nancy Tyler in the computer section."

Hall looked through the doorway, into the first-floor bedroom. The bed was changed, the sheets and blankets taken away, and the mattress folded so the bloodstains didn't show.

"Nancy, Stiggers. I thought you might be working the graveyard. I need something fast. While I hold. It's in the area of labor wars, strikes. The 1910-11 Wobbly... that's International Workers of the World strike against a company in Copper City, Utah. What was the company involved? Is that company still doing business? Yes, I'll hold."

"Baker was the killer who tried to throw me into the Irish sea," Hall said. "That was on the ferry to Rosslare."

"The first I've heard of it," Stiggers said. He moved the receiver closer to his ear. "Yes, Nancy, I'm still here. *New York Times* article, you say? No, I don't want all the details." He listened for a few seconds and nodded. "Greenstock Copper." Stiggers lifted his eyes toward Hall. "Yes, that's the easy one. See what else you've got on Greenstock." A long wait. "You need it narrowed down? Nothing in the *Wall Street Journal*. Going back how far? Maybe there was a takeover or a sale." Stiggers lifted his head toward Hall. "She needs a year. You want to make a guess?"

"A hunch. Try the date the mill town changed from Copper City to Flat Canyon."

Stiggers ran his eyes down the page. "Try 1932, Nancy."

"Could be a new company might want to wipe away the stigma of the Copper City union busting."

"Could be," Stiggers said. "I'm still here, Nancy. That's it. Greenstock takeover by Kennedy Copper. Is Kennedy still listed? The *Journal* again." Stiggers put his hand over the mouthpiece. "Anything else we need to know, Will?" He took his hand from the reciever. "It is still listed. Good."

"Is there a connection between Kennedy Copper and Worldwide Metals?"

Stiggers repeated the question. "Is that right? Rivers did?" Stiggers turned to Hall. "Nancy has put together a file on Worldwide Metals for Rivers. She's getting it now. Go ahead, Nancy. Right. Right. Thank you, Nancy." He broke the connection. "Kennedy Copper is one of ten companies under the Worldwide Metals umbrella."

"Now it makes sense," Hall said.

Stiggers warmed the coffee over a gas flame until tiny bubbles appeared along the sides of the pot. He poured for both of them. "What now, Will?"

"You're in charge."

"Rivers and Moss hadn't briefed me."

"You'd have to take my word for it," Hall said. "My word hasn't been much good around the Company lately."

"Try me." Stiggers sipped the scalding coffee. "I think I can tell if it's the way Rivers and Moss thought."

"Set your mind for Rivers. Moss hadn't had a new thought since 1970."

Stiggers nodded. Hall filled him in on everything that had happened and why, starting with the Costa Verde factions, how Worldwide had supported Marcos and the blackeye the murder of Marcos had given the Company, right on up to the hit on Rivers to prevent him from flushing out the mole in the Company ferret out their man in the Company and take revenge against Worldwide.

"Rivers had a plan?" Stiggers asked.

"Two ideas. Both were intended as a method of telling Worldwide to stay away from Company business. He wanted to warn the people at the top that the Company wouldn't be used and manipulated. One early idea would have been to use the stock market games. Trust busting, S.E.C. investigations of any shady or questionable practices we could uncover. The process might have taken a year or two."

"At least that," Stiggers said.

"The other, the one I think Rivers was leaning toward, would have been some immediate action. Some operation that would have hurt Worldwide, given them a bad lump and the warning at the same time."

"A punitive strike?"

"On that order," Hall said.

"It's got Rivers' touch to it."

"We hadn't settled upon a target. There was the risk of failure if Worldwide had moles in the Company."

"I think I see a gleam in your eye, Will."

"It just came to me. I'm sure that WW Security is responsible for most of the plotting, the roadblocks and the killings." Hall made a face at the coffee. He'd had enough for the night. "They are based in Flat Canyon, Utah. That's where we strike."

"What kind of strike?"

"A wipe-out," Hall said.

"I think the Old Man might go for it."

Hall dumped the coffee dregs. He found the cognac decanter and poured a stiff shot in a water glass. He considered the Old Man, the director of the Company. From all he knew about Bledsoe, it didn't seem likely. "I can't see the Old Man risking it. The F.B.I. wouldn't sit still for it. Worldwide Metals could exert some pressure through the House and Senate."

Stiggers smiled. "Not *that* Old Man. The ex-Old Man."

The ex-Old Man invited them to breakfast. Stiggers and Hall had eaten earlier at the safehouse. "I'd appreciate some coffee, sir," Stiggers said. Hall nodded. The ex-Old man's eyes bored away at him.

Breakfast was placed on a linen-covered table in the solarium, along with two extra cups and saucers, before the old gentleman led them from the living room. His name was Stanford Brewster and he'd walked in the halls of power since he'd been a young man. Now he was probably 75 but he carried himself with the vigor and the erect walk of a man ten or fifteen years younger.

Brewster ate his breakfast slowly while Stiggers filled him in on everything. Now and then he lifted his eyes from his plate and stared at Hall.

Brewster buttered a final thin wedge of toast and nibbled at it, small rat bites. After he swallowed, he touched his mouth with a crumpled linen napkin.

"The bastards," he said. Flat and emotionless but it carried weight. He dropped the napkin beside his plate and stood. "Have another coffee and wait for me in the library."

He marched away. After half-an-hour, Stanford Brewster joined them in the library. He'd changed from a dressing gown to gray slacks and a red sweater "I've made four calls to the city. As you might imagine there is a certain amount of anger about the accident that look the lives of Moss and Rivers and their driver."

"Enough anger, sir?" This from Stiggers.

"More than enough. The last gentleman I spoke with was Winston. You remember Winston?"

"Buck? Yes, sir."

Buck Winston was one of the last of the gentlemen mercenaries. He'd fought in more than half-a-dozen of those small brushfire wars in Africa. Back in 1976, he got tired of war and he returned to Maryland. With some family money added to his pay from those mercenary years, he went into business as an international arms dealer. His "in" with the Company, some of his rivals said, gave him an edge in most arms deals.

Brewster pulled back his sweater cuff and looked at his watch. "Mr. Winston will be here in two hours. He has also offered to recruit and equip twenty-five or even fifty men if we need that many."

Hall put his cold coffee aside. "I think we need some proper intelligence about Flat Canyon."

"In about twenty-four minutes, a satellite will adjust its course so that it will pass over that southwestern part of Utah and begin beaming photos back to NASA," Brewster said. "We should have those photos by courier later this afternoon."

"A night or early morning pass might be valuable as well," Hall said.

"That can be arranged." Brewster circled the ornate desk that was the center of the library. He took a large legal pad from the center desk drawer. "Let's talk manpower," he said. "Men who have debts and loyalty to the Company but are no longer with it."

In twenty minutes, the list stood at twenty-five names.

"Start calling them," Brewster said to Stiggers.

Buck Winston arrived on time, wearing twill trousers, a British shooting sweater and cowboy boots. He had a hard-weathered face and a slim, springy body. After hellos, Brewster locked himself in the library with Winston. Stiggers and Hall were directed to the solarium where soup and sandwiches were being served.

Fifteen minutes later, Winston joined them. "The old man had some calls to make." The butler brought soup and a sandwich to Winston. Winston started his soup, waiting until the butler was gone, and then lowered his spoon. "You know, we need a month to do this properly."

"At least that," Hall said.

Stiggers said he figured on two weeks.

"You know the way he is." Winston tilted his head in the direction of the library. "He wants it in four days. He doesn't want much time to pass between what happened at the safehouse and our reaction to it." Winston spooned bean soup into his mouth. "I've been asked to honcho it. Hall, you're my right arm. Stiggers, you'll stay with us through planning so you'll know what the operation is. Then you go back to the Farm. We want you there when the shit hits the fan so you can control it."

"I'd rather be with you," Ray Stiggers said.

"I can understand your feelings. From what Brewster told me, Rivers thought there might be a leak at the Company. Whatever else he was, Rivers wasn't a fool. I want you there, on top of it. When word of this operation reaches Washington, somebody is going to wig out. The leak is going to feel the heat from Worldwide. I want your eyes there. I want you to pick him like a ripe cherry."

"Alright, Buck."

"A team player this time and a leader the next," Winston said.

Stanford Brewster stopped in the solarium doorway. "The photos have arrived as promised. In fact, even earlier than we'd expected."

CHAPTER FIFTEEN

The series of daytime, satellite photos were lined up across the top of Brewster's desk. Brewster pushed three of the shots aside and drew one toward him. "Not much variation between them," he said.

Winston leaned over the photo. "What time were they taken?"

"Eight a.m. their time," Brewster said. "Give or take a minute or two."

The mining crater caught their attention first. Huge cranes and scoop caterpillars dotted the surface of the crater. Brewster placed a metal ruler over the crater and said, "To scale, I'd say the diameter is about two-point-three miles."

The crater was, according to the photo, to the west of the mining company compound. A road ran along the rim on the north side of the crater. Dump trucks lined this road, pointed toward the east where the railhead was.

"Conveyer belt," Winston said. "Lifts the ore from the mine level to the road. Trucked to the boxcars here." Winston tapped the road and dragged a fingernail along it. "Boxcars and rolling stock here. Targets, I think."

To the east, almost bordering on the open mine, were two clusters of buildings. The road that continued to the railhead dog-legged there and sliced between the two groups of buildings. On the south side of the road, they were low row buildings. "These two," Brewster said, "are probably barracks for the workers. It's going to be hard to estimate how large a work force there is."

"It might not matter," Buck Winston said. "One hundred men or two hundred. I'd doubt any of the working stiffs have access to arms."

"True." Brewster moved the metal ruler. He indicated an L-shaped building. "Probably the mess hall. Notice the wide loading ramps in the elbow of the L. Also, the row of containers, probably for garbage." Brewster turned to Winston. "Your guess as well?"

Winston nodded.

Across the road from the row buildings and the mess hall was an orderly cluster of four buildings. "One of these or maybe two could house the administration and operation units of the mining company. One could be executive apartments or housing. That leaves the one we have to worry about, the WW Security firm. It's going to be important to know which building is Security."

Hall moved forward and looked at the photo closely. "Too bad we can't get an angle to see any communications gear that might be on one of the roofs. That might be the giveaway."

"I might arrange a helicopter pass," Stiggers said.

"Better not," Winston said. "It might worry them."

Hall backed away. "What time is the night fly-by of the satellite?"

"Around three a.m.," Brewster said.

"Midnight their time?" Hall nodded. "Lights ought to tell us what we need to know."

Buck Winston turned and looked at him.

Hall placed a finger on the buildings to the south of the road, the barracks and the mess hall. "At that hour, any lights over here ought to be safety lights. Bathrooms and hallways." His hand shifted to the cluster of four buildings on the other side of the road. "It ought to be about the same here. Minimal lighting for administrative offices and for executive housing. If there is such housing. The busy building, the one showing the most lights, ought to be WW Security."

"A guess," Winston said.

"Let's hold off judgment on this until we see the result of the night fly-by." Brewster dropped the metal ruler on the photo and took a long cigarette from a box on the side of the desk. His hand was pale and shaking. The strain of the day was getting to him. "Let's pinpoint the targets."

"The siding and all the rolling stock," Winston said.

"Equipment," Hall said. "Trucks, dozers, cranes, all heavy machines."

"The administrative building." Brewster touched the cluster of buildings north of the road.

"I want a search of the security files. We take what we want. Then we blow all computers, communications and any arms stores." Hall lifted his eyes from the photo.

Brewster nodded. "I think Mr. Hall should lead a group that deals with WW Security."

"He's owed as much," Buck Winston said.

Hall smiled. "I'll volunteer."

"We done here?" Brewster jammed his cigarette into an ashtray.

"Not yet," Buck Winston said. "There's one question nobody's asked or answered. How many do we kill?"

Hall shook his head. "No blood at all would satisfy me."

"Three of ours are dead," Stiggers said.

Brewster turned the question toward Buck Winston. "You?"

"We kill the ones we have to. An eye for an eye only works if we get the right three eyes. I'm with Hall on this. If we can strike and go and not burn a cap, I could live with that."

"Enough said." Brewster closed the meeting.

The safehouse was, for all intents and purposes, closed. Stiggers sent his man, Bob, on a run to the house to collect Hall's clothing and belongings. Hall spent the night in a room in Brewster's guest wing.

Over breakfast, while Hall and Winston and Brewster ate, they studied the series of photographs from the night fly-by. One building, at the far eastern end of the four-building cluster, revealed a light intensity that exceeded any from the neighboring buildings or the barracks and mess hall across the road.

"That's it," Hall said.

"You willing to bet your ass on it?" Winston said.

"If I have to."

"You have to. You crash the wrong building and you'll give security time to recover."

Hall lifted an eyebrow toward Brewster. "One more day fly-by?"

"I might have used up all the credit I have over there." Brewster studied Hall's face for a long moment. "I can give it my best try."

"I want the best magnification we can get on this four-building cluster on the north side of the road."

Brewster carried his coffee into the library with him. Winston watched him go. "Daytime?"

"I want a good look at the vehicles parked around these buildings."

"Ah." Winston smiled.

After breakfast, Hall rode with Buck Winston to his arms warehouse in Maryland. Huddled over Winston's desk, they drew up a list of explosives and arms for twenty-five men. Ingram M-10 .45 caliber, SAW's that fired the 5.56 mm ball, Browning 50 caliber machine guns, M-21's with the 3-9 Redfield scopes, grenades, explosives in satchel charges and a command detonation system.

"You've got your choice of handguns," Winston said.

On the way from the warehouse, Buck Winston left the list with his foreman. "I want these stacked by the loading door by this evening," he said.

The new day fly-by photos from the satellite might as well have been blow-ups from the photographs from the day before. The resolution was sharp. Hall had the first look at the four-building cluster and backed away from the desk to give the others a chance.

Buck Winston stepped forward. A long stare at the photos and he said, "You're right. Jeeps and Land Rovers. Only a couple of personal cars." He edged his finger away from that building on the far east and touched the other three. "Mainly late model autos and station wagons. No jeeps or Land Rovers in the parking at these three." He lifted the hand and touched the squarish building where the most light had shown during the night fly-by photos. "All that light and now the patrol-type vehicles... this is your security hut."

"It's settled then?" Brewster walked across the library and stopped. His back was to a fireplace. A huge log burned in it. "The next question is when?"

"Hall?" Winston passed the question.

"Today's Wednesday. When will we have the group together?"

"Eighteen have already arrived. They're being housed at a motel down the highway from the warehouse. Seven to go and I've got promises they'll be in the fold by noon tomorrow."

"Do we have time for test-firing? Check-outs with the weapons?" Hall asked.

"Half-a-day," Winston said.

"I say Sunday. I'd rather it was three weeks from this Sunday but..." Hall let it fade. "If we don't have the time, we don't have the time. Friday we coordinate the groups and set the plan in concrete."

Brewster nodded.

"Saturday for travel. We need a C-130 H. A private strip where we can land and three UH-60 Blackhawks to meet us there."

Brewster nodded again.

"We copter in as close to the Flat Canyon mine as we can get," Hall said. "We hike in the rest of the way."

"Best time?" Winston was relaxed, approving.

"We turn it loose just before first light."

It didn't look like a gathering of thugs. It could have been a meeting of stockbrokers and lawyers and successful executives from the top forty companies. Except that the men seemed dressed for hunting and fishing. Jeans and tan cotton slacks, thick wool sweaters and leather jackets, split sheepskins, Korean War issue pea jackets and Vietnam foul weather coats.

The full meeting was held after lunch on Thursday. Stanford Brewster presided. He might have looked out of place in his three-piece gray banker's suit. Not to these men. It was the way all of them remembered him from the old days. Unruffled, cool in every kind of situation.

Buck Winston's warehouse was closed for the afternoon. It was crowded in the lunchroom, surrounded on all sides by drink dispensing boxes and sandwich machines. The tables had been taken by the early arrivals. The others stood against the walls or leaned against the machines.

The preliminaries didn't take long. The reason for the raid and the strike was given. Brewster outlined the basics of the plan. As far as Hall could see, there were no wet eyes for Rivers or Moss. Most of the men didn't know Aaron. The feeling Hall had was that it wasn't anger or revenge that motivated these ex-Company men. It was, instead, a fierce pride.

Earlier, before the meeting, before Brewster arrived, Hall had been at the coffee machine using his last quarter to get himself a cup of the lukewarm liquid. He'd heard one man near him say, "Everybody thinks they can fuck with the Company and walk away from it."

"Laughing and smiling," the other man said.

"It's time the rules got cut in stone," the first man said.

"Washed in the blood of the lambs."

"The sheep," the first man said.

"Three teams," Brewster said now from his position near the doorway. "Ten men in each of two demolition teams. Five worker bees and five riding shotgun in each squad." Brewster paused and looked around the crowded room. "How are you, Franco?"

"Never better, sir." A squat man with dark hair and a five o'clock shadow that looked like ground-in coal dust pushed away from the wall and stepped forward.

"Franco, you and Buck will head these teams. Pick your men."

The selection didn't take long. Franco and Winston could have been choosing men for a softball game. Near the end, there was a hassle over one man but Brewster mediated. "No, Ed Bantry's being held out for Hall's unit."

When the two demolition teams were set, Brewster told Buck and Franco to take them into the warehouse and brief them on the targets and the timing for the strike.

Six men remained in the lunchroom with Hall and Brewster. Brewster introduced Hall to them. The final man to shake Hall's hand was Ed Bantry. "I saved Ed for you. He'll be your second. Anything happens to you, Ed's got to know what you want done at WW Security."

Bantry was a runt of a man, hardly five-five. Wiry and so thin that Hall had the feeling that if Ed turned sideways, he'd disappear.

"Lunchroom's yours," Brewster said. "See you back at the house later." A wave and Brewster left.

Hall said, "Push a couple of those tables together." When they were seated Hall looked from face-to-face. He'd have to get their names straight, in short order. When the chips hit the table Sunday morning there wouldn't be time to hesitate. "Anybody got quarters for the coffee machine?"

Later that afternoon, after the teams were disbanded and the members returned to their rooms at the motel down the highway, Winston and Franco and Hall stood in a snow crusted field behind the arms warehouse. The field wasn't large enough for a full-size mock-up of the Flat Canyon site. Winston argued for scaling it down and using it for a run-through.

Franco, blowing on his hands to keep them warm, seemed withdrawn and disinterested.

Winston paced a fifty-yard track in the snow. "This is the road along the rim of the mine crater. North. Dump trucks use this road to haul the ore to the railhead. We blow the trucks." Winston stopped and waved an arm toward the imaginary crater. "Heavy equipment down there. Cats and cranes and a conveyer belt that brings the ore to the road level. Blow those."

"Right," Franco said. "Anything of value."

"If you've got spare charges," Hall said, "you could blow the road in two or three places as well."

Franco nodded. "We'll arrange to have enough charges."

"After the charges are planted, you form a defensive line and wait. My team will need cover on the way back." Winston paced beyond the fifty-yard track in the snow. "My team reaches the railhead. We set explosives on all the rolling stock and the siding." He turned and paced the dog-leg of the road that curled around the east side of the mine crater. Then he stomped down the snow to form that road that ran between the two groups of buildings. "To the south here, the barracks and the mess hall. I set up a Browning 50 here, to control the road and any entrances and exits from these buildings." Winston stopped and pointed with his left hand to the north side of the road. "Four buildings here. I try to decide which is the admin building. I place charges. After that, I set up a line to cover Hall here." He nodded at Hall.

Hall paced through the road that ran between the buildings. "While two copters are flying you in from the west and placing you as close to the crater as possible, my chopper swings wide and drops my team on a landing site to the east. We hike in from the opposite direction. I set up a Browning 50 at the other end of the road. From there, we cover the mess hall and combine with Buck to neutralize the barracks. I post two men on the street and hit the security building. In there no longer than thirty minutes and out."

Winston moved forward and planted the toe of his cowboy boot in the dog-leg section of the mock road. "I cover until I see Hall leave the security building and heading east. If there's no hitch, if we don't draw fire, I send five of my men back to join you, Franco. I keep only the shotgun riders."

"My turn?" Franco stepped back and stood in the road beside the mining crater. "I cover you, Buck, until you're past me. Then we fall back. You give the order and I blow the whole fucking zoo."

"That's it," Buck said.

On the walk across the field that took them to the parking lot behind the warehouse, Hall noticed that Franco fell behind three or four paces. Hall turned toward him. "Something bothering you?"

"I don't think a run-throuqh on a to-scale mockup is worth snake piss."

"Buck?" Hall waited.

"We scrub it then. Anything else?"

"It sounds too easy. Nothing's that easy. You got a good medic?"

"We'll fly in a Green Beret medic from Bragg. The best."

"That it?" Hall said.

"Now I'm all smiles."

"Keep that thought." Buck put an arm around Franco's shoulders and pulled him level with Hall and himself. "What I hate most is a pessimistic spic."

"Wop you mean," Franco.

"Wop. Spic. They're all the same."

From the gray sky a snow like grains of fine sand pelted them.

CHAPTER SIXTEEN

The C-130 H left Andrews Air Force Base late Saturday afternoon. The grease from the top, all of Stanford Brewster's influence, had the flight ticketed as a training mission for a group of top reserves who were being sent to the Salt Lake City area. "Rapid deployment to control riots and civil disorders," a part of the orders read.

The cases containing the weapons and explosives had been loaded aboard the plane an hour before takeoff by a team from Buck Winston's warehouse.

The twenty-eighth man on the flight was the Green Beret medic from Fort Bragg. A tall silent man who sat alone at the back of the compartment with his medical gear stored on the seat next to him.

Some men slept. Others prowled the Hercules smoking and talking and laughing. Hall dozed part of the time, half-hour naps. Until the waking and sleeping pattern tired him and he forced his eyes open and watched the darkness outside the C-130.

Buck Winston slept the first hour. He awoke fresh and energetic. From that time on, he never seemed to stop moving. He stalked around the compartment. He had a few words for each of the men. Once, when Hall looked toward the back of the plane, he saw Buck seated next to the Green Beret medic. The medic was smiling and nodding his head.

With the time difference, the C-130 bumped down on the out-of-the-way air strip a few minutes before midnight. The flare pots that lit the perimeter of the strip burned just long enough for the plane to touch down and taxi toward the huge tin hanger. Behind the C-130 a pickup truck crept along. Two men on foot snuffed the flare pots and tossed them in the truck bed. In a matter of minutes, the strip was dark except for the lights from inside the hanger.

Winston delegated the unloading and uncrating to Franco. While that was going on, Winston and Hall entered the hanger. The helicopter ground crew, six of them, sat on a dirty blanket and drank coffee and played penny-nickel-dime poker.

"Up there," one of the crewmen said. He hadn't waited for the question.

Buck led the way up the stairs to the ramp that ran along the top of the hanger. Two of the pilots were in sleeping bags. The third one was reading a dogeared paperback novel. When he saw Winston and Hall, he turned down a page to mark his place and stuffed the book in a pocket on the leg of his flight suit. "Bill. Mike. We got company."

The introductions were first name only. Winston lit a Pall Mall and said, "When you get in?"

"This morning," the pilot who'd been reading said.

"You do the recon?"

The pilot nodded. "Soon as we topped off the tanks."

"How is it?"

"Flat and level as a pool table," one of the other pilots said.

"Except for the mine crater. That's a side pocket in a pool table."

"You pick the sites?"

"No trouble there. To the west of the mine I marked a spot half-a-mile from where the crater is. Mike and I can put you down there twenty-five minutes after we take off from here."

The third pilot, the one who'd been reading, bummed a smoke from Winston. "The land to the east of the mine isn't as level as it is to the west. But I think I can get you in and out."

"That's what we need to know. Five-thirty all right with you?"

The three pilots nodded. The pilot who'd been introduced as Mike had his head down for a long moment. Then he lifted it. "Any chance of us finding out what's going on?"

"Better you don't know."

Mike laughed. "I knew there would be days like this."

"The things you do when you take Sam's dollar," Hall said.

"Ain't it true?"

At five-thirty exactly, the three helicopters lifted off from the landing strip and headed southwesterly. For the first twenty minutes they flew in a tight line. At that point, the chopper with Hall and his six men curled away and performed a wide loop to the east.

The first gray light of morning showed on the horizon.

Franco and his team reached their position first. The half mile jog had sweat pouring from his face. Down the road that ran along the north side of the mine crater, in the distance, he watched Buck Winston and his team trot toward the railhead, the siding, and the dim shapes of the buildings.

At six-fifteen on the second, Whispering Bill Thompson, wearing lineman spurs and with a belt looped in place, climbed the telephone pole nearest the defense line Franco had established. Cutters in hand, he waited for the signal from Franco. Another five minutes passed. Franco wanted to give Buck as much time as he could. He waved a hand at Whispering Bill. Bill cut the telephone wires and scooted down the pole.

Whispering Bill discarded the spurs and climbing belt and reclaimed the M-21 Franco was holding for him. He moved forward and joined Mace Curtis, who'd set up his Browning 50 so the road was a killing ground.

"Now," Franco said. Four men climbed down the conveyer belt that led to the bowl center of the mine crater. Each man carried a backpack of satchel charges.

"You. You." Franco pointed at Bates and Cummings.

These two men ran forward, past Mace and Whispering Bill. They carried short trenching shovels. Bates dropped to his knees fifty yards ahead of the defensive line and dug the first of three holes in the hard earth of the road. Cumming swung to his left and crabbed his way along the slope that bordered the road. He planted two charges in the overhang before he returned to the road and unlimbered the Ingram M-10 that he carried slung behind his back. He dropped to one knee beside Whispering Bill and Mace.

Franco walked to the rim of the crater. The four men had reached the surface of the mine. The men split, as if on a signal, and trotted from the base of the conveyer belt. Each man had an assigned area. Franco watched while his men moved to the cats and cranes. A satchel charge was tossed into the cab of each piece of machinery.

Franco checked his watch. On time. On schedule. He swung around and stared down the road. Buck Winston's men had reached the railhead and siding. It was too easy, he thought. A cakewalk of an operation. It made him uneasy. Into every hard strike some shit must fall. It was time for the shit.

Jogging, feeling the discomfort of the run, Buck Winston decided that handball and tennis hadn't maintained the endurance that field time did. He sucked in huge gulps of air and felt his lungs burning.

His team reached the railhead. He waved an arm and five men dropped away and headed for the siding and the rolling stock. Four men carried packs of charges. The other clutched an Ingram M-10. He would bodyguard while the charges were placed.

Buck led the remaining four men of his team down the dog-leg road in the direction of the first cluster of buildings. When he reached the first structure, he pointed at Jilly Mission.

Mission unslung the pack from his shoulders and ran, bent-over, until he stood under the overhang of the building. Mission opened the flap of his pack and dropped two satchel charges against the foundations.

Winston dropped to one knee at the corner of the building. He charged the Ingram M-10 before he turned and pointed a finger at Carter and Briggs.

Carter loped across the road, lugging the Browning 50. Briggs trailed him, the SAW at the ready.

Winston watched while Carter planted the tripod of the Browning 50 facing the end of the first barracks. From there, he commanded both a section of the road between the two sections of building and any movement that might develop from the rear of the barracks.

Joe Paris stood behind Winston, an M-21 braced against the corner of the structure. Mission returned the empty pack to his shoulder and unslung a SAW. He placed his back against the siding, braced the frame metal butt of the weapon against his thigh and jacked a round into the chamber.

Soon, Buck Winston thought. It was time. Then he saw the single file of Hall's team come over the slight rise at the other end of the road. One man, the one who carried the Browning 50, swung away from the file and planted himself in a position that faced the L at the end of the mess hall. A false step, Winston thought, and then another man left the file and trotted away to join the man with the Browning. That was it. That was the way of it.

Good enough. Suddenly, unexpected, he heard the cough and rumble of a jeep that made its turn at the end of the road, from behind the security building. The file of men appeared to melt into the slope. God, the driver of the jeep must be half asleep. Lulled by the boredom of the job, the long peaceful nights.

The jeep passed the security building. The headlights were on low beam. It headed straight for Winston's position. Across the way from Buck, Carter and Briggs flattened themselves and blended into the gray shadows.

"You and me," Winston mouthed at Joe Paris.

Paris nodded.

The chopper touched down on a low section of land about three-quarters of a mile from the company town. Before Hall left the chopper, he checked watches with the pilot. "Start them up in forty-five minutes," he said. "We'll be here by then."

On the run, climbing the slight rise, Bantry remained on Hall's left shoulder. "One more time," Hall said.

"Any files on Costa Verde."

"Yes."

"Marcos."

"Right."

"Files on William K. Hall."

"Yes."

"Files on the Company."

"You've got it all," Hall said.

They reached the crest and started down the slope. Hall trotted forward and touched Timmons on the back. Timmons didn't look around. He broke the file and trotted to the left, the Browning 50 over his shoulder. Timmons had gone twenty yards before Jaime Cline realized he'd missed his assignment. He split away from the file and sprinted after Timmons.

Shit for brains, Hall thought.

Headlights on a low beam sliced the road.

"Down," Hall hissed. The four men with Hall fell to their stomachs, faces in the dirt. Hall swung his head to his left. Timmons was down. Cline was still running. At that moment Timmons lifted his arm and dropped it and Cline sank to his knees and flopped face forward.

The jeep reached the head of the road and made its turn that took it past the front of the security building. It crawled. Twenty miles an hour, Hall thought.

Ed Bantry edged forward on his elbows until he was beside Hall. "This change anything?"

Hall shook his head. "If he reaches the other end of the street, he belongs to Buck."

The jeep slowed before it made a turn to the right onto the dog-leg section of the road. When it went out of sight, Hall got to his knees. Then to his feet. The four men followed him down the slope. Hall angled toward the parking area in front of the security building. He lifted his head. It was just light enough to see the communications tower on top of the roof. Yes, this was the right boy. That was the thumbprint.

Keeping low, spreading as they went, Hall and the four men with him entered the parking area in front of the security building. They crouched, getting their breath, in the shelter of a Land Rover. Hall's arm was coming up, about to point toward Spence, to motion him toward a position on the far side of the steps, when the front door of the security hut opened and a huge man in a tan uniform stood in the doorway, backlighted. He was dragging on a cigarette. He leaned against the doorframe for a count of ten or fifteen. He took a step forward and flipped the cigarette in a high arc. He wheeled and returned to the room, closing the door behind him.

The cigarette cleared the roof of the Land Rover and landed at Hall's feet. Hall waited until the door was closed before he lifted the toe of his boot and mashed the butt.

CHAPTER SEVENTEEN

Buck Winston placed his mouth within an inch of Joe Paris' ear. "Passed on to us."

Paris shifted the M-21. "Now?"

"After he makes the turn."

The jeep slowed when it reached the end of the street. The dimmed headlights swung toward the forward edge of the mine crater. As the jeep turned, the beam turned toward the dogleg and pointed in the direction of the railhead and the siding.

The headlights missed the building corner where Winston and Paris and Mission were placed. Winston touched Paris on the arm. He didn't wait for Paris to move. He was crouched, almost duckwalking behind the tail of the jeep. One hand caught the side of the jeep. He made a long leap forward and placed the barrel of the Ingram M-10 about three inches from the driver's face.

"Brake it," he said.

The driver braked hard. Winston, with a hand on the side of the jeep, was thrown off balance.

The driver rolled away from that side of the jeep and was reaching for something on the seat when Joe Paris said, "Don't do it," and pointed the M-21 at him.

The driver eased away from the passenger seat. His hands moved until they were level with his ears. Steady again, Winston pointed the Ingram at the driver. On the other side of the jeep, Joe Paris cleared the seat of a Dan Wesson .357 and its fancy holster.

"He's yours," Winston said.

Paris stepped into the jeep's passenger seat. "Move it." The guard started the engine and drove down the dog-leg toward the railhead.

Winston returned to the corner of the building. Mission moved aside to make room for him. "Trust me, boy," he whispered down the road, directed at Hall. "You know I handled it. That's why I'm here. Do it now."

For the first time he was sorry they'd decided not to use walkie-talkies. A quiet job was a hard one. Walkie-talkies would have added an element of risk. WW Security might have sophisticated electronic gear that could sweep the area.

"Do it, Hall."

"Buck shortstopped him." Hall lifted the Python. Under his left arm was the Ingram M-10 in the special rig Winston had furnished him. It was almost a fast draw holster. What he was saying to himself was, *even if Buck didn't take him, we can't stay here.*

Ed Bantry charged his Ingram. "Let's do it."

Hall pointed a hand at Spence.

Spence nodded and sprinted for his assigned place on the other side of the stairs that led into the security building.

Low steps. Three of them. Hall avoided them. Never knew when a step might squeak. He caught the hand rail and pulled himself onto the landing with his left hand. He squatted there. A look over his shoulder.

Bantry stood at the bottom step, waiting for his move, Len Gauss and Sly Joyce bunched behind Bantry. Hall straightened his legs. The top half of the door was glassed. When he was stretched to his full height, Hall had a view of the lighted room. The heavy man who'd been in the doorway moments before was now behind a desk. The desk was positioned to the right of the doorway. Straight ahead another man slouched on a sofa, A riot gun was propped against the arm rest, more than a reach and a leap away.

The door opened inward. Hall remembered that from the way the heavy man had closed it behind him. Hall grabbed the door knob. A turn and it was open. He'd been prepared to put a shoulder against it if he had to. He lifted the Python and stepped into the room. As he went, he cleared the door.

The heavy man behind the desk lifted his head. His eyes were sleep-coated. "What the hell …?"

Bantry rammed into the room. His Ingram swung to the left, covering the man on the sofa.

"Easy," Bantry said.

Gauss and Joyce were half a step behind Bantry. Joyce closed the door.

Hall said, "Len," and motioned toward the desk. Gauss circled the desk. He touched the heavy man behind the head with the SAW, to let him know he was there, and backed away two steps.

Joyce didn't wait for orders. He crossed the room and grabbed the riot gun. With that in his hands, he slung the Ingram and jacked a round into the riot gun.

"No games," Hall said.

Sly Joyce waved the riot gun at the man seat on the sofa. "On your belly." The man dropped to his knees and fell forward on his chest. "Hands behind you," Joyce said and he circled the man and placed a hand on his back.

Bantry crossed the room and stood at the man's head. He nodded at Joyce. Joyce put the riot gun aside and took a two-inch wide roll of adhesive tape from a hip pocket. He taped the man's hands and then backed away and taped his ankles together.

"Watch the door," Hall said to Joyce. He didn't wait to see Joyce carry out the command. He headed for the door at the rear of the office. Bantry joined him. Night lights burned in a narrow hallway.

Down the left were neat, small offices. To the right, there was glass paneling. The whole length of that side of the hall was a computer room.

"Charges in there," Hall said. A door straight ahead, at the end of the hall. Hall sprinted in that direction. Behind him, he heard the first thump as Bantry kicked at the locked door.

A staircase behind the door. Hall climbed it at a run. Time was ticking in his head. Lost time. A dark hallway. He found the switches and cut on the overhead banks of light. The man offices. He passed one room with EQUIPMENT-NO ADMITTANCE written on the opaque glass top half. He turned back and tried the knob. Locked. He reversed the Python and hammered the bottom left corner of the glass panel. Huge splinters broke away. He reached in and caught the inner knob and turned it. The door opened. He stepped in and found the light switch. It was the arms room. Riot guns in a row. M-16's. A wall with hooks. On the hooks, handguns of all kinds. Boxes and crates of ammo lining the floor.

Hall heard footsteps in the hall. He backed away from the arms room and swung the Python toward the source of the noise. Bantry trotted down the hall toward him.

"A charge in there," Hall said.

An open door. Hall looked inside. A conference room with a huge polished desk and about a dozen chairs. He went past. Bantry sprinted to catch up with him.

Bantry swung his head to the right. "I'll give that a looksee."

Hall stopped and saw Bantry kicking in a door marked COMMUNICATIONS.

The next door was marked ASSISTANT DIRECTOR. Hall passed that door. He eased to a stop in front of the door marked DIRECTOR. This one. He reared back to give the door a kick directly next to the knob. He stopped and leaned forward. A twist of the knob. The door was unlocked. Now that was careless of them, he thought. He entered the office. The drapes on the far side of the desk were open. He found the cords and drew them closed before he switched on the desk lamp. Just in case.

A bathroom and a shower to the left. A faint scent of shaving lotion. He crossed to the other side of the room. That whole wall was lined with file cabinets. Hall found the "C" file and pulled at it. Locked.

Bantry entered and placed his Ingram on a corner of the desk. "You ought to see that comm room. It's got three-quarters of a million in gear in there."

Hall gave the "C" file another yank. Nothing. Bantry laughed and reached into a knife sheath near the calf of his left leg. He drew out what looked like a miniature version of a crowbar. He stepped around Hall, inserted the tip at the top of the file drawer and gave the blunt end of the tool a whap and a push with all his weight. The lock gave and the file sagged forward.

"Never go anywhere without one of these," Bantry said. He backed away from the "C" file. "I'll get M for Marcos."

Head down, rifling the files. Hall heard another lock break. He didn't look up. Costa Verde, Company, C.I.A. He pulled those files.

"Got Marcos," Bantry said.

"Try United Mining," Hall said.

"Here's H." Bantry inserted the tool and broke the "H" file lock.

In a matter of minutes, Hall and Bantry had a stack of files almost two feet thick. Bantry split the stack and grabbed his Ingram. "Short of time."

"With you." A sudden, unexpected thought. "Crack the J for me."

"Here." Bantry passed him the tool. When the file flew open, Bantry turned his leg toward Hall. Hall slipped the miniature crowbar into the sheath. Bantry nodded at the back pack. "One charge left."

"Leave it there. I'll be right behind you."

As Hall bent over the "J" file he heard Bantry running down the hall.

In the office below it was calm. The heavy man behind the desk had a patch of tape across his mouth and his hands were wrapped behind him. Hall placed his stack of files on the front edge of the desk.

Sly Joyce was beside the door. The riot gun in the crook of one arm. "Quiet on the street," he said.

"Nothing at all?" Hall drew in a deep breath.

"Lights going on in a couple of the barracks rooms." Sly Joyce dipped his head at the stack of files. "Got everything we came for?"

"And more," Hall said. "Ten minutes. We got to haul it."

Bantry opened the door to a closet behind the desk. He reached in and came out with an empty mail sack. He flapped it open and threw in the files he carried. Hall passed his stack of files across the desk to him.

Bantry slung the mail sack over his shoulder. "We leave these two in here?"

Hall hesitated. It was a risk. "Can't leave them. This place is ashes in twelve minutes. We haul them up the slope a ways with us." He crossed to the door and relieved Sly Joyce. "Cut that one's feet free. Take him with you."

Joyce nodded. A few long strides and he stood over the guard who was face-down on the floor beside the sofa. He pulled a knife from his belt and bent over the man. He slashed at the tape that held the man's ankles together.

Sooner or later, Buck Winston knew that somebody would step into the shit. That was the first law. And if there was shit, around you could bet you'd find a footprint in it. That was the second law.

167

It was almost time to withdraw and there was no sign of Will Hall.

Move it, goddam it, he whispered to himself. It was time. It was past time.

And then came the first footprint in the shit. Joe Paris drove the jeep to within five feet of the corner of the building where Winston stood. He left the engine running and jumped from it.

When he was close to Buck, Paris said, "I took the other five men down the road to join Franco."

Good idea. And that was exactly what Buck was about to tell Joe to do when the front door of the admin building opened. A tall, lanky man in a tan WW Security uniform stepped onto the landing and stood there. He carried a riot gun loose in his right hand, the barrel low.

"That you, Milton?"

Buck swept Joe and Mission away, until their backs were flat against the siding. Steps squeaked under the man's weight. He was coming down to the street level.

"Milton, you taking a nap?"

The grind of thick boots on sand. The guard marched toward the corner of the building. Buck cut his eyes toward the Browning 50 position where Carter and Briggs were. They'd seen the guard and flattened to the ground. The Browning muzzle pointed toward the guard, tracking him. So far, the guard probably hadn't glanced in that direction.

Two or three, not more than four steps away from the corner, Buck estimated. He held the Ingram toward Joe and gave it to him, then he reached behind and drew the short Gerber blade from its case next to the holstered Browning 9 mm. Buck held the blade low, angled upward. Waited. He saw the man's boot tip first. Now. He swung away from his hiding place. The blade hitting the man just below his breastbone, centered there and Buck pulled it high and hard. The guard held the riot gun at a high port. He felt the blade and tried to pull away. The knife edge turned and struck a rib. With his last strength the guard tried to ram the riot gun at Buck's head. Buck had stepped against him and the riot gun slammed against his collarbone. Locked together. Buck turned the blade and gave it another hard pull upward. The guard was dying. The last thing he did alive was get off one round from the riot gun. The slugs slammed against the wall of the barracks across the street.

"What the hell was that?" Sly Joyce stopped and pushed the guard he held by the arm onto the sofa. Hall was at the door. Len Gauss and Ed Bantry came from behind the desk and crowded near the door.

Hall couldn't see anything on the street. The angle was bad. It was then he turned his head and saw the guard who was seated in the chair behind the desk.

Sly Joyce had reached the far end of the desk and was about to pass in front of it. Hall saw the heavy guard push his chair forward and push his legs into the space under the desk.

Hall shouted, "Watch it, Sly."

It was a credit to his reflexes and training that Sly could move at all. There wasn't time for him to change directions. He couldn't fall forward to the floor. What he tried was a backwards curl leap. He was in the air, falling backwards, when the twin barrels of the shotgun mounted under the desk went off. The force of the shotgun blast slammed the desk against the heavy guard who'd hit the trip switch with his foot.

It was close, very close. The blast of the shotgun caught Sly's left leg just below the knee and sliced it off to the jagged bone. The force threw him across the room like a rag doll.

The roar in the closed room deafened Hall. He lifted the Python and pointed it at the guard behind the desk. He was too slow. Bantry shouted something and aimed the Ingram M-10. A long burst slapped into the guard and tipped the chair on its side.

Hall lowered the Python and dropped to a knee beside Sly Joyce. He was in shock. "Anybody got morphine?"

"Always," Gauss said. He squatted on the other side of Joyce and opened a kit. He brought out a needle and broke the protective tip away. He jammed it into Sly's shoulder. Hall snaked his belt free and wrapped it around Sly's thigh. He pulled it as tight as he could. Blood had pooled next to the stump. Now the bleeding slowed.

Hall stood. "Len, you got the carry duty first."

Gauss passed him the SAW. He lifted Sly Joyce. As he turned, he looked at the other guard who was watching what was happening with wide eyes. "What about him?"

"Fuck him," Bantry said. He tipped the barrel of the Ingram upward and shot the guard in the face.

Hall looked away. He shoved the Python into the hip holster. He refolded the metal stock of the SAW and aligned the tripod, so it was out of the way. He charged the SAW and nodded at Bantry.

Bantry opened the door and swung it inward. Hall was through the door first. Then Len Gauss carrying Sly Joyce. Bantry followed. As they went down the steps, Spence joined them from his station beside the building.

A window on the second floor of the barracks across the road grated open. A man in a dingy t-shirt leaned on the sill. He backed away and was gone for a few moments. When he returned, he braced what looked to be a .22 rifle on the window casing. He fired twice at Buck Winston. Both rounds were high, slapping against the building.

Winston sheathed the Gerber blade and reached behind him for the Ingram. Joe Paris passed the M-10 to him and then stepped wide of him and fired the M-21 from the hip. Wood splintered from the casement, glass flew, and the man in the window ducked out of sight.

"Movement at the other end of the street," Joe Paris said when he passed Winston. He lowered the SAW and ducked into the cover at the corner of the building.

"Hall?"

"Leaving," Paris said.

"Three minutes," Winston said. "Then we do a bug out."

Joe Paris checked his watch.

Will Hall waved Spence ahead of him. Spence locked hands with Gauss and they formed a carry sling for Sly Joyce. Hall turned and looked down the road when he heard automatic fire. He dropped to one knee. The SAW in place. To his left, facing the end of the mess hall, Timmons and Cline huddled over the Browning 50. Hall lifted a hand, pointed his finger and cocked his thumb.

Timmons waved before he flopped into a prone position. He swung the Browning, tilted it, and sprayed the end of the mess hall.

Hall remained where he was. After the burst of fire from the 50, Timmons looked toward Hall.

Hall waved him up the slope. Timmons and Cline ran past him. When they reached the slope's crest, Timmons stopped and set up the Browning again.

In the distance they could hear the whir of the chopper blades.

"Ours," Buck Winston said when he heard the 50's. He lifted a hand and rubbed his left collarbone. It was swelling, Broken, he thought.

"Time?" Paris asked.

"One minute," Buck said. "Wave Carter and Briggs in."

Joe Paris stepped around Winston. He gave a long, piercing whistle. A wave of his arm and Briggs lifted the Browning 50. He ran toward the cover where Winston, Paris and Mission were. Carter following, covering.

"Crank up the jeep," Winston said.

To the east there was the sound of the chopper starting and catching. Hall's chopper. Time to go.

"Load up," Buck yelled. He remained at the corner of the building and emptied a magazine from the Ingram into the face of the building across from him. Pain from the swelling collarbone stabbed at him. He turned and walked very carefully to the jeep and got into the passenger seat beside Joe Paris. He passed the M-10 behind him to Mission. He lifted his left arm and braced it across his chest. The road was going to be rough.

⚜ ⚜ ⚜

Franco waited at the defensive line he'd established near the end of the road that ran along the north side of the mine crater. Earlier, when Joe Paris had dropped off five men from Buck Winston's team, he'd sent those five and seven of his own men back to the helicopter landing site. Mace Curtis sat behind his Browning 50 mount. Whispering Bill Thompson cradled his M-21 and smoked a short dark twist of a cigar.

There had been firing. It hadn't panicked him. Not with the men they had. Twenty-seven of the best that were outside the Company now. The pros.

A thought came to him. He chuckled to himself. Hell, they ought to do this once a year rather than having a sit-down dinner somewhere.

"Jeep," Whispering Bill said.

"Ours?"

"I think so." Whispering Bill took the M-21 from the crook of his arm. He jacked a round into it, just to be sure. At twenty yards the jeep slowed.

"Hey, we're friendlies," Joe Paris yelled.

The jeep stopped next to Franco. Franco circled it and looked in on Buck Winston. Winston's face was pale and he was sweating. There was blood on the front of Winston's shirt and down his trouser legs. "You alright?"

"A collarbone, I think."

"Move it, Joe." Franco backed away.

"Back for you in a couple," Paris said.

The jeep kicked up fine red dust. It moved away. Franco turned his eyes toward the buildings in the distance. Got to blow it soon. His hand went to the pack slung over his shoulder. The command detonator.

"Let's jog a bit," he said.

Franco gave Mace Curtis and Whispering Bill a fifty-yard lead. Then he turned and trotted after them. They ran in the dust trail left by the jeep.

Three hundred yards past the road and the west edge of the mine crater, Franco stopped and unslung the command detonator. Whispering Bill returned and stood over his shoulder.

"Boom time?" Bill said.

"Bet your ass," Franco said.

The helicopter that carried Hall and his team looped north again and headed to the west. They were to the north and parallel to Flat Canyon when the world below them seemed to explode all at once. Buildings, the railhead and siding, the road and the mine itself.

A reddish yellow dust coned into the sky.

Even miles away, after the three choppers had joined up and headed for the landing strip, the sky behind them looked like an unnatural sunset. A sunset at seven-twenty in the morning.

CHAPTER EIGHTEEN

Stanford Brewster placed the bucket of ice on the drink cart. He poured himself a jigger of single malt scotch and dropped one ice cube into his glass. "Help yourselves, gentlemen."

There was a soft glow to the library. A new log burned in the fireplace.

"I'll mix for you, Buck." Hall stood in front of the row of decanters.

"Cognac straight up," Buck said. The break in his collarbone had been wired in a brief operation at a hospital the Company used. Now he wore a sling that immobilized the arm. He accepted the shot of cognac and nodded his thanks. Hall splashed himself a single malt. He didn't add ice.

"Two hurt?" Brewster asked.

"The other one's bad." Hall had remained at the hospital as long as he could. Brewster wanted a report from the two of them. When he left the hospital, the doctors were trying to save the knee. It was fifty-fifty, touch and go, whether Sly Joyce would lose the knee as well.

"The one's hurt bad … what does he do?"

"Arson investigator in Tampa."

"A good living?" Brewster sipped his scotch and looked over the rim of the glass at Hall.

"He jobs in work for a couple of the big companies. That's eighty to a hundred an hour when he's working. He's got a good reputation."

"The loss of his leg. Will that hurt his work?"

"Only his life," Hall said.

For a moment, Hall thought the old man would flare at him. But Brewster swallowed the words, "At least there were no deaths in our party."

"Amen to that," Buck Winston said.

"I talked to Stiggers this afternoon. The leak in the Company, if there is one, hasn't revealed himself yet.

"Give it time." Buck sipped his brandy.

"Whoever it is will probably play sleeping dog for six or seven months," Hall said. "And then resign."

"You sure?"

"Unless we try a flush and run," Hall said.

"How?"

"Leak the information about the files we took from WW Security. The man we want probably insisted that he be given some kind of code name by WW Security. A man we can't trust probably doesn't trust WW either. He can't be sure his ass is covered. Maybe he'll worry that his name is in the files somewhere."

"I'll talk to Stiggers." Brewster said. "The files are interesting reading."

"I'll bet."

"I'm having selected pages photocopied."

Hall didn't ask the question. He knew the sly fox would tell him anything he needed to know.

"I want the two of you to have lunch with me here tomorrow."

"All right," Buck said.

Hall nodded.

"There's a special reason for the lunch. Do either of you know John Cabot Masters?"

Hall shook his head.

"John Cabot Masters is chairman of the board of Worldwide Metals." Brewster smiled. "I thought we'd open his closet for him and rattle the bones."

"Fun," Buck said.

Hall laughed. It did sound like a fun way to spend part of an afternoon.

The table was set for four in the solarium.

In one corner of the room was a table that hadn't been there before. It didn't seem to serve any special function. There was, however, a silver ice bucket on one side of it in which there was a decanter of Wyborowa vodka. What seemed odd to Hall were the chair and the leather-covered folder.

Hall and Winston took their pre-lunch drinks in the library. Stanford Brewster waited alone in the living room for John Cabot Masters. After greeting Masters, Brewster led him to the solarium.

Two appetizers had been prepared. On one tray there was thinly sliced smoked salmon, rounds of a coarse black bread, a tub of softened butter and a pepper mill. The other tray held a large container of Beluga caviar, as well as toast points, chopped egg and grated onion.

"I've had the salmon prepared a special way," Brewster said. "A man in Scotland smokes it over a mixture of ferns and saw-dust and sprays it from time to time during the process with a mist of rum."

"It looks delicious," Master said. He was a tall man with a flat, elongated face and eyes that were almost the color of a slate blackboard.

"I swear by the Beluga." Brewster selected a toast corner and spooned about ten dollars' worth of Beluga on it. He placed it on a small dish and poured a shot of the Polish vodka into a chilled glass. He ate the Beluga and washed it down with the almost icy vodka. "However, you may prefer the salmon. You may have become attached to it during your visit to Ireland."

"Ireland?" John Cabot Masters raised his eyebrows.

"The Keep in Kinsale is a nice place," Brewster said.

Masters spread a dark round of bread with butter, topped it with smoked salmon and added a sprinkle of freshly ground pepper. He had his back to Brewster the whole time. Brewster backed away. He stopped in the doorway.

"I have a few matters to discuss with my other luncheon guests. Rude of me, I know, but I think you might occupy your time with a read of the materials I've placed in the folder there. I think you'll find it interesting. Will you forgive me if I'm gone exactly ten minutes? That's precisely how long I think the reading will take."

"I'm afraid I didn't come here to …"

"Indulge an old man's fancy," Brewster said. "Please." He stood in the doorway until a puzzled John Cabot Masters seated himself at the table to one side of the solarium and opened the leather-covered folder.

Stanford Brewster checked his watch as soon as he entered the library. "He's reading."

There was a second bowl of Beluga and the garnishes. It was on a tray on Brewster's desk. A decanter of Wyborowa vodka was packed in ice on the liquor cart. Brewster took chilled glasses from the freezer under the cart. He poured vodka for the three of them. "I've made one other preparation. I've told my man to alert me if Mr. Masters decides to leave before lunch."

"You think he might?" Hall didn't especially care for caviar. He spread a token serving on toast and added grated onion.

Brewster shook his head. "He'll remain. I don't think he will gain anything if he leaves before we play the rest of our cards."

Hall ate the caviar and washed it down with vodka. He poured a second vodka and held it until it warmed a few degrees. The first vodka had numbed his throat.

❈ ❈ ❈

John Cabot Masters waited for them in the solarium. The leather-covered folder was closed on the table and the chair pushed in until the back touched the table's edge. He was pouring a vodka for himself when Brewster entered and began his introductions.

Buck Winston first. Masters stared at the sling Buck wore but he didn't ask about it.

The real surprise was reserved for the introduction of Hall.

"Hall...?"

"William Keith," Hall said.

"I see." Masters said.

Brewster's man entered and cleared away the Beluga, the smoked salmon and the decanter of Polish vodka. He returned with another ice bucket in which a 1977 Muscadet rested. After the four were seated, Brewster's man served lunch. Crepes stuffed with huge chunks of crabmeat, braised lettuce done in the French manner and a mushroom and spinach salad. The Muscadet was crisp and fairly dry. When they finished the first bottle, a 1979 Muscadet was placed in the ice bucket.

Over a glass of the 1979, John Cabot Masters said, "The 1979 lacks a certain something."

Brewster agreed. "I think I miscalculated when I settled upon the order. I suppose we should have tried the 1979 first."

The plates cleared away, Brewster's man served rich dark coffee and a Jean Danflou Armagnac. A sip of the Armagnac and Brewster shook his head. "I'm afraid an Armagnac this smooth and aged somehow defeats the purpose of an Armagnac."

"It lacks a certain razor blade sharpness," Masters said.

Brewster nodded.

Hall listened with half a mind. Sooner or later, he knew, they would get down to business. He sipped the coffee and rolled the aged Armagnac on his tongue. The other part of him thought about the one file he had withheld from the stack given to Stanford

Brewster. That slim file was packed under his shirts in his suitcase upstairs in the guest wing. A file from the "J" cabinet. That impulse. That thought that had floated to the top of his mind at the last moment when he'd been in the WW Security director's office. In one sense, there was regret for that impulse. One part of him wished that he'd remained on the proper track and hadn't wavered.

Brewster's man poured refills of coffee and placed the Jean Danflou on the center of the table. He closed the solarium doors on his way out.

It was time to begin.

"I've seen nothing in the papers," Brewster said. "But I have heard rumors of some kind of disaster at your Utah open mine at Flat Canyon. I understand it rated about a 3.7 on the earthquake scale."

"Was it recorded?"

Smiling, Brewster shook his head. "An opening move."

"I see." Master nodded his head in the direction of the leather-covered folder. "It is an interesting fiction."

"Not fiction," Brewster said. "Your designation of this partial selection from the files as a fiction is a fiction itself."

John Cabot Masters set his jaw in a hard line. He seemed unwilling to argue the point any longer.

Buck Winston leaned toward the center of the table and lifted the bottle of Armagnac "Have there been any estimates of the damages at Flat Canyon?"

"It's a bit early for that." Masters shrugged his shoulders. "It might go as high as fifteen or twenty million. Of course, that is without figuring the interruption to the mining. The mine will be out of production for at least three months."

"A tidy sum." Buck nodded at Hall.

Hall smiled. "It *is* a tidy sum."

"Was there any indication of the cause for the explosions?" Brewster asked Masters.

"We suspect there was carelessness in the handling of explosive charges used in our mining operation," Masters said. "The man in charge of that aspect of the work at Flat Canyon would have been discharged by now. However, he was unlucky enough to get himself killed during the accident."

"He might be called lucky," Brewster said. "I understand that Worldwide does not have much tolerance for mistakes."

"A business like ours can hardly afford the luxury of incompetence."

"Does that attitude extend all the way to the top of the corporate ladder?" Brewster sipped his dark coffee. There was the hint of a smile on his lips.

"It is a judgment our stockholders will probably make at our next full meeting," Masters said stiffly.

Brewster's man entered and stood near the doorway until Brewster noticed him and nodded. "There is a telephone call for Mr. Masters, sir. The caller insists it is extremely urgent."

Brewster stood. "You can take the call in the library." He led Masters from the solarium. When he returned a few seconds later alone, he was smiling.

"I think Mr. Masters is about the receive the second part of the message."

"I don't think Buck and I have been briefed," Hall said.

"Stiggers couldn't go west with you. He invented a way to busy himself while you were gone."

Masters returned before Brewster could continue with his explanation. He was flushed and perspiring. "I'm afraid it was important. I've been called away. I enjoyed lunch and our conversation."

"As we did," Brewster said.

After goodbyes in the solarium, Brewster walked as for as the driveway with John Cabot Masters. He returned, chilled and blowing on his hands to warm them.

"This way, gentlemen." He led them into the library. Brewster circled the desk. He took a small key from his pocket and unlocked a desk drawer on the right side. He opened the drawer. Hall stood behind him and looked down at a small tape recorder.

Brewster reversed the tape. He found the beginning of the conversation and played it:

"John?"

"Yes," Masters said.

"It's Archer.

"Archer Finster," Brewster said. "The number two man at Worldwide."

"All hell has broken loose at on Wall Street. Every few minutes there's a new rumor about the events at Flat Canyon."

"It will even out," Masters said.

"There's been heavy selling in Kennedy Copper."

"It was to be expected under the circumstances."

"There's even a rumor that the S.E.C. is looking at Worldwide. I think it was to do with the July takeover of…"

"Shut up. Archer. I am not sure how safe this phone is."

Brewster pulled a pad toward him. Hall watched while he wrote "July takeover?" in an exact even hand.

"Sorry, John."

"Let's keep our heads. You say the selling is in Kennedy Copper? The volumne?"

"It's approaching a million shares."

"Concentrated buying?"

"Not concentrated," Archer said.

"Any pattern in the buying?"

"It appears to be spread. No big buy."

"I'll be in the office in about two hours. Prepare some kind of statement about Flat Canyon. And use whatever source you have to discover if the S.E.C. is really serious about the investigation of Worldwide."

"Hurry back." Archer said.

The tape stopped with the click of the broken connection. Brewster closed the drawer and locked it. He leaned forward and touched the pad with a finger. "Interesting bit of information, don't you think?"

"You were scatter shooting?" Buck said.

Brewster nodded. "And now we have a target." He lifted the phone and placed it closer to him. He dialed the Farm number. "Brewster," he said. "Zebra four, Charlie two, Charlie one, zebra five." Brewster drummed his fingers on the desk top while he waited. "Yes, let me speak with Ray Stiggers." A brief wait. "Brewster here. Yes, Masters just left. While he was here, he had a telephone conversation with Archer Finster. Something in their talk might be helpful to us. Have your people look into a July takeover Worldwide was involved with. I think we'll find what we need for the S.E.C. investigation." Brewster closed his eyes, listening, "Yes, they're here."

Hall said, "I'd like a word with Ray."

Brewster passed the phone to Hall. He turned to Buck, "Another coffee?"

The library door closed behind them as the two men walked out.

"I'm heading south again tonight or early in the morning." Hall said.

"Give my best to Denise. I assume I can expect her resignation from the Company in the next few days."

"Is that what you want?"

"You're misunderstanding me. If Rivers had faith in her as an agent, then so do I. It's her call. Any idea which way she'll go?"

"No, I don't." Hall said and it was true.

"How about you? Can I talk you into coming back?"

"I like it out here in the wind," Hall said. "However, there is one matter I'd like to discuss with you. How about a couple of late drinks at the Madison Hill Bar and Grill?"

"How late?"

"Eleven o'clock. I'll meet you there."

"We waited for you," Brewster said.

The table in the solarium had been cleared, the linen cloth replaced by a mat on which the coffee service rested. Hall took a chair and received the fresh cup of coffee Brewster poured for him.

"By now, or by noon tomorrow," Brewster said, "John Cabot Masters will be congratulating himself on having weathered that little teapot tempest with the Kennedy Copper stock."

"You don't foresee any real damage?" Hall said.

"Kennedy Copper will recover today's losses and perhaps even gain a point or two."

"Then I don't see the point."

Brewster dipped his head toward Buck Winston. "Do you have a figure on expenses for our western expedition?"

"Anywhere from half-a-million to a million. I can have those exact figures in a day or two."

"I'll expect them," Brewster said. "From my estimate, buying low and selling high tomorrow, our stock manipulation should profit us in the area of two to three million. Perhaps more, perhaps less."

"I like that," Buck said with a big grin.

"Stiggers thought you might." Brewster smiled. "It seems a slightly warped justice that Kennedy Copper and their stockholders are going to foot the bill."

"It leaves a surplus," Winston said.

"Yes?"

"Our team did this with no expectation of pay," Buck said.

"Twenty-five thousand a man? Is that fair?"

"Fair enough," Buck said.

THE SPY IN A BOX

"Maybe we ought to talk with an insurance company." Hall sipped his coffee. "How much is a leg worth?"

"A hundred thousand?" Brewster look toward Buck Winston.

"A hundred and twenty-five," Buck said. "I'll feel better with empty hands."

"One hundred and fifty," Hall said. "I'm in the wind and don't need the money."

"Settled then?" Brewster looked from face to face.

The three men nodded at the same time. It was settled. A bright cold sun flooded the solarium.

He called Denise in Chapel Hill. "How's the weather down there?"

"Don't you talk to me about weather," she said. "Tell me how you are."

"It's done." It was a partial lie but he didn't want to explain. "I'm going to New York in the morning to pick up the BMW that's in storage. I'll take my time driving down. Maybe stay overnight somewhere Tuesday night."

"I'll see you Wednesday then?"

"That house in Blowing Rock. The one you wanted to see. How about cutting a few classes?"

"You know I will."

"A long weekend in the mountains. How does that sound to you?"

"Perfect," Denise said.

He had no idea where the relationship would go with Denise but he knew he'd find a way to end it, with no hard feelings, if she stayed with the Company. Hall didn't want to be in bed with them, literally or figuratively, any longer.

"Got a pencil?" He gave her John Mix's address, where the key to the house could be picked up and they said their good-byes.

The next call was to John Mix in Blowing Rock, telling him to start up the water and power again, give Denise the key, and show her the way to the house.

At eight that evening, after an early dinner with Stanford Brewster, Hall said his goodbye. Brewster's man drove Hall into Washington. Hall checked into a motel a few blocks from the Madison Hill Bar and Grill.

He watched television until a quarter of eleven and then he took the "J" file from his suitcase. He removed the pages and folded them into a thick wad. With those stuffed in his parka pocket, and the Python .357 next to them, he caught a cab outside the motel and directed the driver to the Madison Hill.

Ray Stiggers and his shadow hadn't arrived yet. Hall stopped in the doorway and had his look around. A good crowd, he thought. The Madison Hill was doing well. Not like in the old days when Bilbo first bought the place. Hard times then.

The cocktail waitress met Hall in the aisle and wanted to play hostess. Hall said he'd take a place at the bar. He reached the stool at the far end of the bar and stood there, about to remove his parka.

At that moment, Bilbo backed out of the kitchen, a plate in each hand. Sandwiches for the late eaters. "That goddam Carlos is in the sauce..."

He saw Hall and almost dropped both plates. He steadied himself, grinned and placed the plates on the bar. "It's you. Jesus Christ, I thought..." He grabbed Hall by the shoulders and hugged him. His hip banged against the Python and he said, "Ouch," and backed away. "Man, that smarts."

The cocktail waitress pounced on the sandwiches and hurried away with them.

"What does a man have to do to get a drink in a place like this?" Hall asked.

"First one is on the house." Bilbo poured the Jack Daniels Black. It was a stiff drink. He poured about half that much for himself and leaned an elbow on the bar. "That trouble you were in…?"

Bilbo let his voice trail off.

"Done," Hall said. "I'm halfway to my porch on the side of the mountain."

"Pissing off that porch…"

"A mile down," Hall said.

"That's the life."

"Cheers." Hall drank.

"Bad about those people. Rivers and Moss. I read about it in the *Post*."

"You ever meet Rivers?" The Jack Daniels warmed the pit of his stomach.

"Once. Franklin brought him in. I had a feeling it wasn't quite his kind of place. It wasn't fit for a prince."

"That's it."

"Or a titled Englishman. Lord, those tweeds."

Stiggers and his bonebreaker Bob had arrived a few minutes later.

"Sit down, Ray," Hall said. "Here's somebody I want you to meet."

Stiggers eased into the stool on Hall's left. Bob moved to the end of the bar and stood there, on Hall's right.

"First time here?" Bilbo extended his hand.

"Yes."

"First time here the first drink is on me. Your pleasure?"

"A beer," Stiggers said.

"You?" Bilbo turned to the bonebreaker.

"He doesn't drink," Stiggers said. "A coffee, if that's possible."

"You've got it." Bilbo opened a Molson and put it on the bar in front of Stiggers. He waved down the waitress and ordered a coffee. Then he slid a glass toward Stiggers.

"I don't think I'm doing my manners," Hall said. "This is Jackson. Better known as Bilbo to his friends." Stiggers nodded. "And this is Ray Stiggers."

The waitress placed a coffee in front of Bob and moved away.

"You own this place, Bilbo?" Stiggers asked.

"Me and the bank."

"But he's had some help paying the bills," Hall said. "He's been earning extra money, tax-free, working for Worldwide Security."

"He's shitting you. I don't do security work. This is the only job I have," Bilbo said, patting the bar. "Crusty bartender."

Hall reached into the pocket of the parka. He closed his hand over the wad of pages there and drew them out. He took his time unfolding the paper.

"These are from the Worldwide Security files at Flat Canyon." He slid the pages to his left toward Stiggers. "What we can say in Bilbo's favor is that he didn't find them, they found him. Here he was with a struggling bar, trying to make the payments, and some of us young Turks began hanging out here, running off our mouths. It started with a couple of hundred here and there from Worldwide Security for seemingly harmless information. A profile on me before I headed to South America, for example. When I got moved to Costa Verde, the Worldwide people knew everything about me, from my shoe size to my political leanings, thanks to Bilbo."

The waitress pushed in on the other side of Bilbo. "Two scotch rocks."

Bilbo robotically scooped ice into a couple of glasses. He placed shot glasses on the tray and poured from the bar scotch bottle. But his hand was shaking.

Hall waited until the waitress stepped away from the bar before continuing. "Worldwide knew enough to manipulate me through Paul Marcos."

"That in here?" Stiggers touched the pages on the bar.

"In brief. The profile Bilbo did on me is in my file."

"What put you on him?" Stiggers looked past Hall at his bonebreaker.

The bonebreaker hadn't touched his coffee since the talk got serious. He was poised.

Bilbo saw the look. Without thinking, Bilbo lifted a bar towel and wiped his face. He stopped, looked at the cloth and dropped it in a bucket under the bar. It was over for him and he knew it.

"It's been rattling around in my head since the ninja boy made his try at me upstairs. At the time, I thought Boyle, doing his ninja act, was from the Company. Two men knew I was here. Franklin and Bilbo. I thought the try came through information from Franklin. No reason to suspect Bilbo of having any part in it. And now it adds up. Boyle had to get by the security alarms, had to know which room I'd be sleeping in, and had to get past the locked door into my room." Hall looked at Bilbo. "He had the keys, didn't he? A key that got him past the alarm and into my room. Maybe the keys were still in the door when you came down the hall after you heard the shot. Maybe they were on Boyle. You had plenty of time to find them before housekeeping arrived, between the time I left and they got here."

Bilbo didn't answer. He placed the bottle of Jack Daniels on the bar and poured some into a shot glass. Hall waited until he released the bottle. Then he poured a stiff shot for himself.

"Another thing probably in your favor. They wanted you to do the job on me and you wouldn't. Right?"

Bilbo dipped his head. A short nod. He lifted the shot glass and poured the whiskey down his throat in one swallow.

"Not in your favor. You got enough booze in me to drown a wino. It should have been easy for Boyle, except he had to try his silly ninja act."

"What cinched it for you?" Stiggers asked Hall. "Why did you go to the 'J' file at Worldwide Security?"

"Because of what Rivers screamed just before he died at the safehouse."

"What?" Bilbo raised his head.

"The house was wired and a tape was running," Hall explained to Bilbo. "We have the whole strike recorded. Rivers managed to say what sounded like *bib*. He was trying to say Bilbo. But he got his tongue twisted in his terror."

Stiggers stared at Bilbo. "You were there?"

Bilbo didn't answer, so Hall did.

"I think Worldwide called in their marker on him." He turned to Jackson. "What did they say? 'You've been paid well and now you earn it.' Something like that?" Bilbo didn't answer. "Ah, maybe a dollop of blackmail as well. 'Do it or we pass your name around and you're out there in the cold by yourself.'"

Hall could tell from the expression on Bilbo's face that he'd scored a direct hit.

"Why use him instead of a professional?" Stiggers pushed the beer bottle away.

"Time was short. Had to get it done before Rivers and Moss could get their plots and plans underway. Had to finish what they'd started in Ireland. Rivers was too smart for Worldwide to allow him to follow a scent for long."

Stiggers looked at Bilbo. "Time to close up for the night."

More likely forever. Bilbo knew it, but there was nothing he could do now. He waved a hand at the cocktail waitress.

"Annie, tell everybody we're closing early tonight. The last drink is on the house." Bilbo's voice was hoarse, raspy.

"Hey, we got a good crowd and the tips ..." she began, but he cut her off sharply.

"Do it, Annie. Now."

"Geez, who pissed in your porridge?" she said and marched off in a huff to give the customers the news.

Hall stood. There was half-an-inch of the Jack Daniels left in his glass. He tossed it back and tapped the glass on the bar top. He looked at Bilbo.

"The way we figure it, there were two men at the safe house. Man Number One got Aaron on the front steps. Man Number Two chased Moss into the kitchen and got him. Man Number One then went into the first-floor bedroom and killed Rivers. You were Man Number One. Were those killings your first, Bilbo?"

"No," Bilbo's voice was almost a whisper.

Hall nodded. He didn't ask who else Bilbo had killed or the circumstances. Whether it was on a battle field or in a dark alley. If it was for God and Country or for himself.

"Aaron was an easy kill," Hall said. "He didn't see it coming. Why was that?"

"His guard was down," Bilbo said. "He thought I was his relief from the Company."

The only way Bilbo could know that was if he'd been in contact with the mole in the Company. Hall turned and looked at Stiggers, who nodded. He'd had the same thought. Hall stepped away from the bar. Stiggers followed him. They stood a distance from Bilbo.

"You won't have to squeeze Bilbo too hard to find out who Worldwide's man at the Company is and who worked with him that night at the safe house," Hall said.

Stiggers nodded. "He's given up."

"It wouldn't surprise me if the mole and the shooter were the same man."

"You're probably right," Stiggers said. "You did good work."

"Just trying to get out of the box I was put in."

"You want to know the name of the mole when we get it?"

"No," Hall said. "It doesn't mean a thing to me."

"How about how it ends for them?"

Hall knew how it would end. So did Bilbo, unless he had more information to barter in exchange for a longer life expectancy. Perhaps that was what Bilbo was signaling to Stiggers by answering Hall's question and essentially admitting he knew the mole. More games. It was tiring.

"Not really," Hall said. "I'm done."

"You don't have to be," Stiggers said.

"Yes, I do."

Hall walked out of Madison Hill Bar and Grill without another look at Bilbo Jackson. The man was already dead to him and buried in an unmarked grave. Good riddance.

It was raining. An ice rain. Hall stood on the curb for a minute or two. No cab passed. His buttoned his parka and lifted the hood. He walked the six or seven blocks to his motel.

The rain tapped on his motel window all night long.

ABOUT THE AUTHOR

Ralph Dennis isn't a household name...but he should be. He is widely considered among crime writers as a master of the genre, denied the recognition he deserved because his twelve *Hardman* books, which are beloved and highly sought-after collectables now, were poorly packaged in the 1970s by Popular Library as a cheap men's action-adventure paperbacks with numbered titles.

Even so, some top critics saw past the cheesy covers and noticed that he was producing work as good as John D. MacDonald, Raymond Chandler, Chester Himes, Dashiell Hammett, and Ross MacDonald.

The *New York Times* praised the *Hardman* novels for "expert writing, plotting, and an unusual degree of sensitivity. Dennis has mastered the genre and supplied top entertainment." The *Philadelphia Daily News* proclaimed *Hardman* "the best series around, but they've got such terrible covers..."

Unfortunately, Popular Library didn't take the hint and continued to present the series like hack work, dooming the novels to a short shelf-life and obscurity...except among generations of crime writers, like novelist Joe R. Lansdale (the *Hap & Leonard* series) and screenwriter Shane Black (the *Lethal Weapon* movies), who've kept Dennis' legacy alive through word-of-mouth and by acknowledging his influence on their stellar work.

Ralph Dennis wrote three other novels that were published outside of the *Hardman* series – revised and re-released by Brash Books under the new titles *The War Heist* (aka *MacTaggart's*

War), *A Talent for Killing* (aka *Dead Man's Game*), and *The Broken Fixer* (aka *Atlanta*) — but he wasn't able to reach the wide audience, or gain the critical acclaim, that he deserved during his lifetime.

He was born in 1931 in Sumter, South Carolina, and received a Masters degree from University of North Carolina, where he later taught film and television writing after serving a stint in the Navy. At the time of his death in 1988, he was working at a bookstore in Atlanta and had a file cabinet full of unpublished novels.